THE BEAST WITHIN

THE JOURNEY OF A LOST SOUL IN ADDICTION AND HOW HE FOUND REDEMPTION THROUGH HIS OWN ANGELS AND DEMONS

DANIEL THOMAS JR.

ISBN-13: 978-1-9763-2302-7

I dedicate this book to the memories of my two cousins and my friend. I wasn't there for you in life, but I will be there for you in your passing. I will not allow you to be forgotten. May the three of you rest in peace. It's well deserved.

CONTENTS

NOTE FROM THE AUTHOR: ADDICTION 101 1

CHAPTER 1 3

CHAPTER 2 5

CHAPTER 3 9

CHAPTER 4 13

CHAPTER 5 23

CHAPTER 6 29

CHAPTER 7 33

CHAPTER 8 39

CHAPTER 9 49

CHAPTER 10 55

CHAPTER 11 61

CHAPTER 12 69

CHAPTER 13 77

CHAPTER 14.. 85

CHAPTER 15.. 91

CHAPTER 16.. 97

CHAPTER 17.. 99

CHAPTER 18.. 105

CHAPTER 19.. 111

CHAPTER 20.. 121

CHAPTER 21.. 131

CHAPTER 22.. 135

THANK YOU 137

WANT MORE?... 139

A QUICK FAVOR PLEASE? 141

ABOUT THE AUTHOR... 143

NOTE FROM THE AUTHOR: ADDICTION 101

Welcome. You're about to immerse yourself in the tale of a tortured mind, the brain at its most devious. Is this a story of a substance abuser and his struggles within? Or is it a tale of good versus evil, with an addict as the main character? Perhaps a mix of both.

Even if you don't want to admit it, our pleasure center rules our behavior. I smoked my first cigarette at ten, had my first drink at eleven, and smoked weed at fourteen. My friends and I, throughout our lives, tried every drug known to mankind. Hell, there were even a few we made up ourselves. Addiction is a prevalent yet misunderstood disease. If you believe you're impervious or totally in control, you're sadly mistaken. Depression and suicide coexist with addiction. It's a lonely affliction. The main course comes with three sides, the triumvirate of pain, misery, and death.

If you haven't been, let's say, privy to any of this, then you're either lying or in denial. Addiction is always lurking just around the corner. It's in your own home, at your neighbors', in our schools, and down the block. Whether you choose to believe or not, it's ingrained in society. We're all capable of unleashing the monster, *the Beast within*. Some do and some don't—no reason, it just happens. Is it possible to be a victim of circumstance? Can evil work the same way? Is it in all of us? Maybe. Most people seem good, but not everyone is.

The story you're about to read is fiction, based on fact. We're going to call it faction, JT's faction. The names were changed to protect the innocent, skanks need not apply. In my life, I've personally experienced major addiction, bullying, loneliness, depression, and suicide among my family and friends. It was even part of my own thought process. So far, to this point, I've survived it all. Humor and an ability to laugh at myself have gotten me through many tough times. I'm cynical, sarcastic, and the funniest mofo I know. It doesn't always translate to others, but still, I crack myself up. Other than drugs, music has been the best friend I've ever had. Music is the one thing that gives but never takes. It's the most amazing therapy, and I could not live without it.

CHAPTER 1

I t is July of 1975. In the Middle East, at an undisclosed location, sits the tallest building in the world. Security at the front gate is like no other, and only the invited dare to gain entry. On the top floor, there is a clean one-bedroom apartment. Plush white shag covers the floor. Across from the door, a set of white drapes is strung the entire length of the wall, with no visible support. Though there are no fixtures or electrical outlets, the light never fades. The living room, filled with incandescence, gives off a warm glow. A lone table, created from the Tree of Knowledge, sits with two chairs. There is a pair of iconic figures at the table. They are musing over life, death, and the game that is set out before them.

"Why do you protect your queen with such vigor?"

"A king is nothing without his queen, my Father. The knights are noble warriors, always by her side."

"We have been playing this game for many years. You do realize the bishops and rooks are more valuable than the knights?"

"They have more ability, not necessarily more value. The rooks are not to be trusted, always sliding around and never taking responsibility for the chaos they create. And the bishops? They always have an angle, and they're a bit stuffy for my taste."

Our Father lets out an uproarious laugh that shakes the foundation. "Michael, I do so love our time together. You never fail to amuse, your heart always being in the right place. I have even seen you sacrifice your king just to save a pawn."

"Are not the pawns the most valuable pieces on the board, my Father?"

"A most unique perspective that should be shared by everyone. Indeed, in life, they truly are. You have rescued many pawns through the centuries, Michael, and I now have a special task for you. There is a soul being delivered to a small town in Michigan today. I am assigning you to be his guardian angel, as this one will be needed sometime in the future."

"I am both honored and perplexed, Lord. What makes this one so special? You haven't assigned me a specific human in over two hundred years."

"Jeremiah will be needed to keep the balance. Fate will see to it, but it will not be easy. This one will be quite a handful, even for you."

"As you wish, my Father."

"One more thing, Michael …"

"Yes, my Lord?"

"Send for my Son. I need some competition … CHECKMATE!"

CHAPTER 2

On an interstate, somewhere in mid-Michigan, a car roars beyond the speed limit. The destination is a farming community called Siam located in the southwest portion of the mitten. It is May 20, 2016.

We're returning from Mackinac Island, cruising along I-75 at one hundred miles an hour. My girlfriend's black-on-black '89 Corvette is no ordinary car. Melchiah Immerson, my Egyptian beauty, is no ordinary woman. Her wavy shoulder-length black hair and deep blue eyes make Mel irresistible. She handles this rocket like a maniac and thinks it's funny to pin me in my seat.

"I'm only in third gear, baby." Mel gets this sly grin. "Let's check out the rest."

With that, my head feels like it's been sucked back by an industrial Shop-Vac. This is a 382-horse Callaway. The Vette seems made for her inner spirit. I glance at the speedometer, close my eyes, and say a prayer … swear it read 122.

"There's more under the hood, JT." She laughs this crazy cackle. "Hope you're ready!" She hits it hard as I close my eyes again, focusing only on her squeals of ecstasy. It feels like we've been launched into space. This woman ain't right, and I love it! There is an upside, as the sex is off the hook after a ride in Mel's car.

The vehicle finally starts to slow. I open my eyes and glance over—back down to 100, Mel's cruising speed. Now she's got the look, her eyes giving away her intentions.

"Let's find a rest area."

My grin turns into a big smile, knowing what awaits.

We roll up the ramp and back onto the highway—at cruising speed, of course.

"It always pays to carry a sleeping bag, eh, babe?"

I laugh. "It's about the only thing that will fit in this car besides us." Time to get my head right, so I pull out a greenstick. I crack the window and spark it up. Damn, Holy Grail Kush, tasty as they come. "Wanna hit this thing, baby?"

"You know I don't smoke." She laughs. "But I love the way it smells."

I stretch out and fall into my head. We've been up on the island for a few days attending my buddy Dave's funeral. I was asked to be one of the pallbearers and was proud to accept. Dave was my age, 41, and a successful lawyer. He had it all until he met painkillers. In two years, he lost his health, his sanity … and his life. My friend Dave committed suicide. One day it all finally rolled up on him, and he shot himself. If crushing anguish and self-loathing aren't enough, it can get horribly worse. Running out of opiates … withdrawal … sickening, horrifying withdrawal. Try taking 15 to 20 pills a day for months and then running out, unable to find ANYTHING. After a couple hours, it's crazy. I once went a stretch of 36 while praying to God to take my life. Dave couldn't wait for God, so he took matters into his own hands. I wasn't there for him. I'm so sorry, Dave. Please forgive me, my friend.

God, he is a good man, let him rest in peace, please let him into Heaven. Please, God … he has a good soul.

It was great to have Mel by my side. I was a mess and she stood by me, my rock of strength. As the grief was piling on top of me, she got stronger.

"Bet you're hungry, JT. Let's stop at the diner."

I look over and smile. "I could use some breakfast."

CHAPTER 3

I'm glad we've decided to stop and grab some food. Funeral aside, just haven't been right lately, and I'm not ready to go home yet. Window's down and the cool breeze feels good across my face, even at one hundred miles an hour.

Mel turns, her face scrunched. "Can you turn down the radio, baby?"

Shinedown's "Sound of Madness" is playing. Love this stuff.

"Hey! Baby, you okay? You listening to me?"

The book on pain, if he wrote it, I've memorized it. I'm a headbanger from way back. Can't make a mistake once and be done with it, hell no, not me. Gotta keep banging my head on the wall … over and over and over! There must be others who can relate. Bang your head once, it doesn't take long for the pain to fade. You forget a bit about how much it hurt. You think, "Maybe it'll be okay now—didn't leave a mark last time." That voice in your head tells you, "Try it again, you'll be fine, listen to me." So, BANG! You do it again. This time it leaves a mark, maybe even a scar. With enough time that voice comes back, "I'm stiiiill heeere, try it again, you'll be okay, trust me." So, SLAM! This time it leaves nothing … it starts taking. First it takes a piece of your mind, then a piece of your soul … that's the sound of madness.

Feeling strange lately, like I'm not alone in my own body. And the voices, yes, the voices! They started by entering my dreams, familiar yet

9

terrifying. My waking hours are no better now. I'm hearing something on occasion. Garbled noise? Words barely within reach? Can't help but feel I brought this all on myself. Must be my Catholic upbringing, default to guilt. Not even sure what—

"Babe!" Wow, snapped back to reality, and Bully is cranking.

I have a real problem with people that prey on the weak. Tearing other humans down just to make themselves feel powerful. Dominating them mentally and physically. I get enraged when I focus on that.

"Are you even in this car with me?"

"Sorry, baby, haven't been sleeping well. I'm out of it today."

"What's really bothering you? It's more than the funeral. It's been going on for months. Please open up to me."

"I'm fine, no worries."

"You never let me in."

Let her in? Careful what you ask for—What the hell was that?

"Did you just say something, Mel?"

"Nooo, I'm done talking to you."

Don't believe that for a second.

"Baby."

See.

"Don't shut me out."

Back in my head. I thought I could make myself better, cure my own ills. I am in control. I'm in control! No, I'm not. I'm well beyond the scars. I'm so damn frustrated! God, do you really hate me? Give me strength! Please!

"JT, are you okay? Why are you grabbing your chest!"

"Can't take a full breath. What's going on?"

"You're stressing yourself out again, baby! Oh, hell, you dropped the joint. Find it before it burns the carpet!"

"Where did it roll? What the hell!" I'm clenching my teeth so tight my ass hurts.

"Baby, try and relax."

"I want out of this car!" My face starts twisting. "God, I hate my life!"

Mel is just staring at me, the most incredible look on her face. "Now you're scaring me. What's going on? I feel like I can't even talk to you."

That doesn't seem to stop her.

"Baby, your behavior has gotten crazy."

"Pfff, my behavior? Really? I've been fighting demons my whole life."

Mel swings left, and we pull into the parking lot. I shoot her a look. "Thank God, we're here. Let's get out of this freaking car and eat."

She slams the door. "Maybe that's your problem, too much faith in God." Mel's face gets an ugly twist.

"Easy on that door, bitch. You wouldn't want to hurt your precious car. And you can keep your atheist attitude to yourself! Maybe you should leave. I'll get a ride home."

"JT, please, can we just go in and eat. I'm sorry, I should know better." She runs her fingers through my hair, smiles, and snuggles up closer. "What's wrong with your shoulder? You were rubbing it the other day too."

"It's my collarbone. I get a relentless tingling from deep inside." I shake my head. "No matter how I rub it, I can't quite get to the itch."

And something strange always happens right after.

"Doesn't make any sense." I'm starting to feel a bit calmer. "Let's go in and eat."

CHAPTER 4

Ahh, my very own small-town diner. You know the kind—been there for decades, chipped paint on the walls with a permanently dirty floor. There's always the smell of grease, with a sweaty guy in a dirty white T-shirt cooking eggs. A row of stools commands the front counter. Booths with permanent stains on red seat cushions ring the outer walls. Tables, all in a row, run down the middle. Well, this ain't it, but it used to be. A fire two years ago gutted the place and burned it to the ground. Now it looks exactly like before, but everything is brand spanking new. Even the sweaty guy doing the cooking, Hal, bought some new T-shirts. He insisted everything be rebuilt the same as his father had it done.

The smell of coffee, eggs, and bacon hits me like a wave. Mmmm, what could smell better than bacon? Weed, for sure weed.

Rho, one of the waitresses, looks up while taking an order. "Hey, JT. Find a table. Be with you two in a minute."

"Thanks, Rhona's a punk rocker, coffee us up."

I get this dadwhoppy to the back of my head with a laugh. "Grab a table, J-man, and chuttuppa uface."

"Sheena's got nothing on you, Sis. Hurry up with that coffee." I'm getting the middle finger head scratch with a huge smile as she bounces by. Mel's got one hand on her hip, head tilted, and copping this irritated lean.

"Rhona's my best friend, baby, relax. And everyone loves the Ramones. She's my little punk rocker. It fits, at least in my brain."

Mel gives me an eye roll with a side of "Whatever."

That kinda pisses me off. "I've about had it with your petty jealousy. Rhona is like my little sister. You've always had a hair up your ass about her."

Mel's face softens, and she slides her body next to mine. Running her hand across my shoulder, she caresses the back of my neck. "JT, I'm sorry. You two are close, and it makes me a wee bit crazy at times. Forgive me?"

I hate it when she does this. Instantly, I forget what I was mad about. All I can think is how good she makes me feel, this warmth surging through me, right to my heart. She flashes her beautiful smile, flicks her wavy black hair back, and focuses those deep blue eyes on mine. "I love you, JT."

That arrow just went deeper than my heart—it went right to my soul. It's as though someone burrowed into my brain and built this woman to my exact specs. I'm lost in a wave of flowing emotion. "I love you too, Mel."

As we walk toward the back, I see a big man with hulking shoulders sitting at one of the tables. Looks like he always gets up on the wrong side, and he's staring right at me. I'm feeling a little violated. Got some crazy salt-and-pepper hair sticking out from under his ball cap, and he's missing a few cutters. Seems very familiar. Why do I know him?

His face is turned up in an ugly sneer, and he's hawking me as I move by. I'm rubbing my collarbone. My stride slows and irritation builds. Finally, I look right at him. "You got a problem, Gomer?"

He brushes me off with a hand wave and head shake. "Just keep moving and let me finish my eggs."

Mel's pulling on my arm as she slides into the booth. "You don't want to mess with that guy."

"Do you know him?" I'm stopped dead in my tracks.

"Babe, sit down. You're losing the color in your face!"

I've got a flutter going in my chest. "Haven't felt this in a long time, Mel, butterflies dancing around my heart. I almost need to hide. Damn, I'm losing it." I'm struck by a pang of sickness. "Ooh, my stomach, it's twisting. My arms don't feel right, the skin … feels like it's rolling off!"

Something turns my head back toward … that man. He's perv-smirkin' and staring me down. His eyes! They're festering and gray! I'm waiting for them to roll back and his jaws to unlock.

Blowing me a kiss, he says, "Just for you, Jeremiah. Enjoy."

My head starts to go fuzzy, and my knees buckle. Mel pops off the bench and tries to hold me up. "Baby, what's going on?"

I whisper, "Something's telling me to move down a couple tables, like maybe all the way to the back."

As we move farther down, I can hear that douche laughing. It's an arrogant I'm-better-than-you laugh, and it's raising the hair on my arms. A flicker of adrenaline lights me up.

Turning around, I stare right back. Anger joins the party and voices its opinion, "Maybe you need a good throat chop to go with your eggs!"

"JT, don't do this!" Mel's hanging on to my shoulders.

"Quit dragging me, stop!"

Dickhead drops his fork and stands up. I stop, now three feet from his table, and we're locked in a thousand-mile stare down. Mel steps between me and the table. "Baby, please … I've never seen you like this! Forget it, let's just sit down."

For some reason, I can't. Inside my head something starts to make sense. Legs locked and coiled, I'm jarred out of my gaze.

"Here you go! Coffee black for you, JT. Cream and sugar for you, sweetie. But only if you're seated." Rho is giving me her look, and it breaks the standoff.

"No problem here, sis."

The arrogant man speaks. "J-man, cute name. Your problem is that you are a child in a man's world."

"What the eff are you jawing about now?"

"Heard your junkie buddy Dave blew his brains out."

Never spend time telling someone you're gonna kick their ass, just do it. I explode with a punch. And it's going ... nowhere? My body is moving backward, and I spin my head. A mountain dressed in coveralls has caught my arm mid-punch. "Oh hey, Jake. How ya doing? Mind letting go of me?" My huge neighbor, Jake, is giving me a look of disapproval.

"I suppose that's your giant of a son holding back the rest of me." I turn the other cheek and smile. "Hey, Laz, how you been?"

"Good, JT, and yourself?"

I laugh. "I've been better."

"He's got it coming, but it ain't worth going to jail over this asshole."

Hal has come out from the kitchen and made his presence known. He's about 150 pounds of sinewy wire that's wrapped pretty tight. No human wants any part of him when he's fired up.

"Goddammit, Willard! What have I told you? Don't be causing any shit around my diner! No one talks that ugly in here. Now finish eating and get out of my place!"

Jake and Laz release their bear hug grip, and the three of us start laughing.

"Jake, is that Willard Little?"

"Yes sir, JT, that it is."

Willard sits back down, doesn't say another word, and goes back to his food.

Hal grins and struts over, much like a rooster that has defended his coop. Putting his arm around me, he gives me a caring smile. "Dave was a good kid, Jeremiah. We all loved him around here. Both of you guys."

I feel a little fatherly advice coming, but it's not what I'm expecting. "It's best if you can avoid Willard. I don't trust him, and neither should you. He's pure evil."

Before I can answer, Hal turns and heads back to the grill. "Damn, Jake, that just gave me chills."

"Lazarus, why don't you go across the street and fill up the truck. I need five minutes to talk to JT." This isn't helping the bumps growing on my arms.

"Jake, we can go sit in the booth with Mel and talk." I glance over to see Mel and Laz trading glares as he walks out of the diner.

Jake, his gaze also focused on that silent exchange, whispers, "Let's just talk alone, JT."

We retreat to an empty table. Jake's a longtime neighbor and family friend. Big Jake, we call him, huge man with a soft smile. He reminds everybody of The Duke.

"This is tough for me to talk about, JT, and I know it's rough for you." Jake swallows hard and continues. "Thinking back a few years to your barn, I couldn't help but believe Willard had something to do with it." Jake could see the flames from his place and had made it over as the firemen were pulling up.

"Jake, I just can't …" My voice trails off as I stare at the floor.

"I know, Jeremiah, just listen. I remember some talk a long time ago about trouble between your family and Willard's. The gossip has since died out, but there was a feud going on. I just want you to watch your back around him."

"My brother couldn't stand him, Jake. Jonathan said he thought he was hot shit coming out of high school. And then, going to Cheater U in Columbus to play football? My brother said they deserve what they get with him."

"Willard had no respect for anyone, still doesn't." Jake is nodding his head as if agreeing with himself. "He wanted everything handed to him."

"I remember. Damn, Jake, wasn't he drafted in the first round?"

Jake starts laughing at the absurdity. "He only played a few years with the big boys before he was pretty much blackballed. He was linked to steroid use, but that was only the tip. Along the way, he left a trail of battered and abused women. Eventually, he came back here. Willard got married somewhere along the way."

Out of the corner of my eye, I catch Rho waving at me. "My food's up, Jake. I appreciate the talk. Maybe I'll stop by sometime and we can talk again."

"You're welcome anytime. You know that. But one more thing, and please don't hate on me for it."

"Spit it out, Jake." I chuckle. "You're not gonna hurt my feelings."

"People around here aren't too fond of Melchiah. She's not the same person when you're not around. Her and Laz have had a few public spats."

"Wow, seriously? Laz is a big teddy bear. He gets along with everyone. What happened with those two?"

"He wouldn't ever tell me." Jake shifts his weight, causing the poor chair some distress. "When I pressed him, all he would say was, 'Dad, she doesn't live by the same set of rules the rest of us do.'"

"I get the gist, Jake. You don't ever have to mince words with me." My hand disappears into his as we shake and do the half-hug backslap.

My head's lost in the conversation with Jake when I sit down with Mel. I do get the gist; this is God-fearing country out here. We have a multitude of Christian sects and a Muslim community. We all share the common belief that there's a power greater than ourselves. We all believe in peace. But I can see Mel taunting, testing, talking crap. She's been doing that with me lately. It's an ugly side that seems to be emerging more and more.

Everything settles, but my eyes won't leave Willard. He must know I'm looking at him. It feels so obvious, but I can't stop.

Mel breaks the silence. "Sooo, that must have been quite a talk you and Jake just had."

"Just catching up." Mistrust is tingling in my brain. "What's up with you and Laz? Don't get along?"

Mel cackles with surprise. "Oh, let me guess. Daddy doesn't like my attitude? That dumb old plowboy needs to get off his pulpit."

"What happened today, Mel? Someone piss in your Cheerios?"

"Baby, please." She takes my hands and runs hers up my arms, gently pulling me closer. "It's been a tough week for both of us." Brushing her face across mine, she whispers in my ear, "I love you, Jeremiah. Let's take a breath and start today over."

What is it with this woman? I can't stay mad. "Okay, babe, let's finish eating and get out of here."

Sis comes by with more coffee as I'm looking up again at the other table.

"All these years and Willard hasn't changed a bet." Rhona moved here from Scotland when she was a little girl. I love it when her accent forces its way back in. "He's alder and gained weight, but he's still the seme, a complete asshole. That man should be in jail or hell for what he's done."

"Rho, what happened to his wife? I heard a few years ago she died."

"That rat bastard preyed on her weaknesses. Kristie was the most beautiful girl, cheerleader, homecoming queen, full of life. He wore her down to the point she started drinking and couldn't stop. He's a total control freak. Gev her some beatdowns too."

He beat her? The context of what Jake and Hal said is starting to mesh. I pull into my head, growing angry. Beat a woman? I'm gritting my teeth and getting pissed. It doesn't even feel like I can control it, and maybe I don't want to.

"They had two kids. She went into recovery and was doing good. Willard totally mind-screwed her and drove her back to the bottle. He divorced Kristie and got custody of the kids."

I'm hardly listening anymore, having gone somewhere deep into my head, thinking about going all William Wallace on this piece of excrement. You know the scene; he rides into this dude's house on his horse, takes the ball and chain, and slams it on the dude's head! I'm feeling a bit evil myself and liking it. Something's fueling this, almost like a Vicodin rage. I'm biting the inside of my lip, thinking about it . . . Just effin slam this piece of shit, right to the head! Leave him happy for the rest of his life, totally lobotomized! My anger is focused. Line up the small of his back and slam! Leave him in a wheelchair for life. God, I can almost feel it! Let's see him bully people now!

"JT, wecanmakethishappen."

I'm so far away in angerland, I swear I heard my brother. I've got so much rage I'm biting a hole in my lip. I feel the blood trickling down the side of my chin.

"Kristie died from complications."

"She died from what?"

"Complications, JT, from the alcohol and Willard."

Mel is suddenly startled. "Oh shit, baby! You're bleeding."

I get Mel calmed down and we finish eating. We get up to leave and see one of the other waitresses, Tracey, crying. Melchiah goes over and puts her arm around Tracey.

I find Rhona. "Yo, Sissy, what's up with Trace?" Been calling Rho that since she was little.

"When Willard left, he bitched her out. Told her she was a horseshit waitress who needs to learn to take care of the man she's servicing."

Tracey is one of the sweetest people I know. She's a bigger girl who's got curves in all the right places. Her long autumn-blonde hair accents her high cheekbones, and she's very pretty to boot. We got together when she started working here. After about a month she was getting too close, so I had to end the relationship. It was a bad time for me, as I was barely out of recovery. At that time, I couldn't even take care of myself, let alone anyone else. Shortly after that, I met Melchiah Immerson, in the woods of all places, and the rest is history. All the barriers came down, almost immediately, and I still don't know why. What a difference a day makes, eh?

"Baby." Mel struts over. "Now I'm sorry I got in your way. Willard needs a lesson in manners! He even told Tracey she's a fat pig!"

It's so easy for me to fall back into my head. Again, I'm focusing on pain, lots of pain. Tracey's a beautiful woman, a wonderful person, and a damn good waitress. Willard's the pig, the pig who needs to be led to slaughter, like all the other skanks in this world. Pain turns to anger, anger to adrenaline, adrenaline to focus … then I can focus on more pain.

"That's an intense look, JT." Sissy laughs. "But that man deserves a good ass-kickin'."

"Don't worry, Rho, karma has a way about it. God has a special place for people like him."

"Yesveryspecial."

"Well, I'm glad you agree, sis."

Rhona gets this sly grin. "I didn't say anything, JT, but I do agree. And my ancestor does as well. He enjoys a good flailing."

A sizzling chill runs up my spine. Sissy, her auburn hair in a ponytail, hops away. This little lady is quite unusual.

As we sit in the car, I get this sensation of calm. This is so soothing that I almost moan. Haven't felt this good in months. I turn the radio on, and Linkin Park's "No More Sorrow" is playing. I love his scream, so I turn it up. I can relate to the emotion in this song. I can be deeply moved by music. It's got me thinking about going home, rolling one up, and jammin' out.

CHAPTER 5

"You must be feeling better. You're smiling."

"First time in a long time the weight's gone."

Can't explain, but damn I feel good. "It's like something great is going to happen for a change. It's a beautiful spring day, sky's clear, and the sun's shining. How does one make a good day better?"

My baby gives me a knowing nod and smile.

"Mel, I need a fix."

"To the rescue shelter it is. JT needs his dog fix." Mel laughs. "How many are you going to bring home this time?"

"They all break my heart, but I'm still not ready. I can't replace Bronco yet. That dog was more stubborn than me. He made it seventeen years. Outlived all my dogs. Right now, I just need some hugs."

We don't get but about five miles down the road before the traffic stops us.

"JT, I see a bunch of flashing lights up ahead. There's police, fire, and an ambulance. What happened here?"

"I don't know, baby, but it doesn't seem we're going anywhere. Let's get out and find Cappy. He's got to be here."

Captain Eugene Davis is ex-marine, sniper intensity, and has the buzz cut to match. When I was in my teens, no matter what trouble I was getting into, Cappy would be there to bust my ass. Captain Davis would take me for a ride, give me a talking to, and then drop me off at home. Before I could get out of the squad car, Cappy would laugh every time and say, "All you need, JT, is a good haircut. That's all you need!" Damn marine. Good thing for me, he and my old man were tight.

Mel and I are out of the car and walking up on a pile of twisted metal that used to be a pickup. The road is all taped off, and the state popos are just starting their investigation. I see Cappy off to the side and wander over.

"JT, how've you been?"

"Apparently better than whoever was in the middle of this."

"That's for sure. You missed it by about 20 minutes—craziest thing ever. The driver was going about 60 miles an hour, turned and swerved to the right real hard. It was like he was trying to avoid something in the road."

"Probably a deer."

"Well, that's the thing. Witnesses swear there was nothing in the road in front of Willard."

I lose my breath and grab my chest. Feels like I took a hit of some harsh weed and can't empty my lungs fast enough. "What! What did you say?"

"Witnesses are saying there was nothing—"

"No, not that. The name, the name—did you say Willard?"

"Yeah, the driver was Willard Little." Cappy adjusts his sunglasses and folds his arms. "You remember him, don't you?"

We almost had a throwdown in the diner. This is turning surreal. "Will- Willard Lit- Little?"

"You okay, JT? Don't feel bad about this. If anyone deserved it, Willard was the one. He was an animal."

Now, here's the strangest part. I'm not getting anything crazy. In fact, it feels almost … soothing.

"I had my own run-ins with Willard. That man never wanted to buckle up. Said he didn't need any damn seat belt. Must have written him half a dozen tickets. Arrogant bastard didn't care—used to tear 'em up right in front of me." Cap grins shit-eatin' style. "He might have made it unscathed if he had been belted in."

I seem to be getting some pleasure from this. What does that say about me?

A whisper brushes my ear, *"Jerrimiiaahhh."*

Jolted, I spin my head around.

"Hey, JT, what's going on man? You're looking kinda funny."

"Did you hear that, Cappy?"

"Hear what?"

"Nothing, never mind. What about being belted in?"

Cap gives me his famous chin rub and head tilt. I can sense some cop stuff going on in there. He lets it go and continues. "When Willard swerved, he hit the guardrail and was catapulted out through the windshield."

Not sure what's going on, but I'm starting to smile.

"He flew like the devil and slammed headfirst on the pavement. The truck flipped a 360, and the front tire landed like a sledgehammer, right in the middle of his back."

Almost can't contain my giddiness. This isn't right, what am I thinking? "Damn, that must have been quite a mess."

Cappy gives this big sigh and shakes his head, like he's in disbelief. "Haven't told you the craziest part yet. Willard's alive. He should be spread out all over the road, but he's in one piece, sort of."

This should be sending wild shivers all through me, but it's quite the opposite. My world has slowed. I notice the breeze. A gentle warmth brushes across my face. Is this tranquility?

"His spinal cord was crushed, and he's gonna be in a wheelchair the rest of his life. The paramedics said when Willard landed on his head, the trauma was significant, but they won't be sure until a scan is done. It's almost like he got a damn lobotomy."

For the first time in months, I'm taking consecutive deep breaths, filling my head with life-giving peace. This is almost exciting. At the same time, I'm horrified, and yet ... not.

"Gotta say, JT, this is one time karma got it right. That sonbitch gonna be ohsohappy the rest of his miserable life. He won't know any different."

"Tell you what, Cap, if karma gets it right, he'll know." I walk away, infused with energy, my legs full of spring. How can I be reacting this way?

Mel is talking to one of the deputies, Samari Tanson. Sammy was my brother's best friend. He always tried to be there for me after Jonathan died. Sammy even pulled me out of the bar, on occasion, and took me home. One time, we didn't make it to my place. Somewhere toward the end of a fifth and fourteen vikes, I felt a grab on my shoulder. "JT, let's get you out of here. You're letting the guilt rip you to shreds. This is too much, even for you. JT, JT!"

This 5'9," 170 lb. guy threw my 200 lbs. of dead weight over his shoulder and bolted out the bar doors. I woke up—four hours and a stomach pump later—in the ER. Samari was sitting next to my bed. He got this huge smile, then his face got serious. "Dude, you need help."

Mel sees me and comes running. Her eyes are wide open with this look of shock.

"Baby." Her voice is quivering. "*It was Willard Little.*"

"I know, Mel. Let's get out of here."

I sit back in the passenger side and tilt the seat back. I stretch out my legs and put my hands behind my head. Mmmm, my back cracks like it's never done. It's amazing how comfortable this seat is. Can't believe I've never noticed before.

"JT, I'm really freaked out right now."

I'm drifting into pure serenity. It's been a while since I can remember feeling this good. It's like taking the best drug ever. This might be one worth chasing.

"Hey, gorgeous, you know how we were rocking it out at the rest stop?"

Mel gets this sly grin, while her eyes peruse my body. She giggles. "Yeeess?"

"We can go to the shelter later. Right now, let's go home."

She turns her eyes back to the road and hammers down the accelerator, the grin turning into a big smile. The Callaway screams as I drift back into my head, body and mind united. I'm engulfed in this total sense of calm, just floating on clouds.

"*When you are focused and your mind is quiet, you hear us as one.*"

I don't even have to ask; Mel doesn't hear a thing.

CHAPTER 6

I walk out of the bedroom and kick back on the couch. Reaching for the jar, I look over at Mel. "Hey, babe, toss me my Zig-Zags. They're right there on the table."

"Here ya go. Whatcha got going?"

"Fresh Gorilla Glue, from the East Side."

"East Side of what?"

Mel was born in Canada. Her family moved down to the Upper Peninsula when she was young. Mel hadn't been south of the bridge until eight months ago. "I forget babe, you're not from Michigan. This is from the East Side of Detroit, St. Clair Shores area. This lady is one of the best growers I've come across."

"That's a long way to go. Can't you find this stuff any closer?"

"Not this strain, and it's never too far to add spice to your life. When I go out there, I stop at the Eastern Market in Detroit. That's where I get the 'special' tea—you know, that funky-ass smelling shit." Can't help but laugh. Everyone in the store knows when the barrel is open.

"Okay, baby." Mel's laughing too. "You and your Gorilla have a good time. Pretty sure you're going to get glued to the couch. I'm heading over to Tracey's. I'll see you tonight."

"Cool. Love you."

"Love you too, babe."

I roll one the size of my little finger and fire it up. After a bit, I set it down and fall deep into my head. I'm taken back to the island …

I've been to plenty of funerals but never experienced anything quite like this. System of a Down's "Lonely Day" is playing in my brain. The hearse is entirely black, including the spoked wooden wheels. Our driver pops the reins, and with a jerk we start rolling … *klippityclop klippity-cloppity klippityclop.* I stare straight ahead at the hearse, expecting to see Dave's soul sitting on the back, begging me to help him. God, please let my friend rest in peace. Help him find the Light.

As we roll down the street, activity slowly ceases. Tourists freeze as if they are doing a slow-motion wave in reverse. Busy sidewalks now turn to stone as people stare. We make it to the church at the edge of town, and I'm drowning in my own thoughts. As the horses slow to a halt, I think about Dave's family. To a person, they had no idea he was so far gone with his addiction. We addicts have perfected the art of keeping those close to us in denial. Hell, we keep ourselves in denial. We lie to ourselves more than we lie to the world.

The definition of addiction—insanity on a daily basis, wanting to live and yet believing death is the better option. We live only for the jones, telling people what they want to hear so they will leave us alone … alone to take care of the craving in our brains, the craving in our bodies. It's insanity at its purist; crazy would be an upgrade. Who else could put a positive spin on the dumbest ideas ever uttered, ever thought? Snort this, swallow that, inject this into yourself. We become experts at pushing our bodies and minds to the brink … of madness? Death? Spiritual genocide? Yes, yes, and yes.

I roll out of my own fog. Man, enough of that, time for some music. I turn on Audioslave, "Show Me How to Live," and grab the J from the ashtray. I need to forget for a while, so I give it a spark. My mind starts moving toward Willard. That had to be the weirdest coincidence in history, with me thinking about slamming that asshat, and then his crash.

Wheelchair, really? Did I do that?

Oh, shit no, JT, you're just effin high.

But I don't believe in coincidence, only fate.

You were hearing the voices.

That just means I'm bin material.

But what about the head injury? Lobotomy?

Poor choice of words, okay?

But Cappy said the paramedics said—

STOP!

I'm so effin confused. The voice said ... hell, it talked to me three times! Willard got hammered ... after I ... enough, enough, ENOUGH.

It makes no damn sense, but I know what does—finishing this joint. Mel can wake me when she gets home.

CHAPTER 7

"Just drop me off over there."

"You sure you don't want me to come in and stay, baby?"

"Look, Mel, we've talked this through, and I want to talk to Doc alone."

Back to not sleeping, full throttle anxiety, and no peace of mind. A month ago, things were getting better, then the dreams started again. The voices are getting stronger. I'm seeing faces talking to me, family I've never met, dead long before my birth. I'm starting to lose my grip, laughing to no one in particular. As if I had a grip to begin with. Man, I'm tired. Hopefully Doc found something in all the tests he put me through last week and can fix it.

"Mr. Treadway, the doctor will see you now."

I've been treated by Doc all my life, and I don't recognize this nurse.

"Follow me, JT, follow us." Wha— did her voice change?

"What was that ... um, Miss? I'm sorry, not sure of your name. I don't think we've met yet."

"Oh, you know us."

"My name's Kristie."

Us? What? She's walking fast. Can't catch up. Need to see her face. Who is Kristie?

"You'll be in exam room 12."

*"Yes, twelve, we **are twelve**, you will see."*

How far is this? I don't remember more than six rooms.

"Will you please slow down, Miss?"

How long is this hall? I need to see her face. My heart's starting to flutter. Seems a little dark down here. Doesn't anyone pay the electric bills? The lights are dim. Wait, what happened to the lights?

"Miss! Hey! Please … stop!"

Whoa, it feels like I walked into the chill of a meat locker. The tingling in my skin crawls up through the back of my neck! Thump, thump, thump. Jesus … my heart's gonna burst! I start to run, but the walls are getting closer! I lunge and manage to grab the nurse. "Miss!"

As she spins around, all I see are her eyes. They are dark and hollow. She speaks in a guttural tone, but it's Mel's voice, "I said my name is Kristie."

Can't stop staring into her eyes.

"We are twelve."

"This is room 12." She points to a door … it opens … I turn to run … I'm frozen! I try to move my feet, but I'm sliding on my heels like a 300-lb. lineman is pushing me into the darkness. There's a light in the distance, and someone's there. Peering in, I see a man sitting with his back to me.

My eyes grow wide … he's in a wheelchair! I step into the room, and it feels like there's a thousand butterflies in my chest! Sucking for air, I step closer. The stench of rotten eggs fills my nose. He spins the wheelchair around! The top of his head is misshapen, a jagged scar running across his forehead. I meet his eyes. They are *festering and gray*.

This can't be … what am I seeing? OH, MY GOD IT'S—

"Mr. Treadway."

No no no!

"Mr. Treadway." My eyes pop open, and I about fall out of the chair.

"I'm so sorry, Mr. Treadway, I didn't know you were sleeping. I didn't mean to startle you. The doctor will see you now."

"JT, how have you been?"

"Okay."

"How are you sleeping?"

"I'm not."

"Eating?"

"Not enough."

"Getting out of the house?"

"No."

"Exercising?"

"No."

"JT, this isn't healthy."

"Well, you're a regular House, aren't ya?"

We try to keep a straight face, but it's not possible, and we both bust out laughing. "Thanks, Doc, I feel better after that." I can always count on Dr. Riley for a smile and a laugh.

This man knows me well, too well for my own good. Doc's real name is Dr. James Riley. He's in his mid-sixties, with short brown hair that's speckled with gray. This tenacious five-foot-ten Irishman played basketball at Central Michigan University. After shattering the all-time scoring records, he moved on to U of M med school and came back here a doctor. He wanted to stay home and serve the people of Siam. I remember when I was 20, I was playing pickup ball, and Doc would come and join us. At 45 years of age, he was still unstoppable. His dizzying array of fades and sweeping hook shots made us look foolish. He would laugh the whole time and talk trash. When we were done, bent over and gassed, he would be standing there ready for more. Doc would say, "Same time next week, boys?" and walk away laughing.

"Let's talk about your test results."

"You mean results from your torture devices? Who can possibly go 40 minutes without moving? Without drugs? That's asking a lot, Doc." I chuckle. "You could have given me Valium or something."

"JT, don't even joke about that. Twice into recovery isn't enough? Third time's a charm? It could be three strikes and you're out."

"Sometimes I need to joke about it, Doc. That way it stays fresh. I wear my addiction in my peripheral. It always hangs about eye level, just off to my right. I never lose sight of it."

Doc flashes me a big smile and gives me a hug. "Good boy, JT." Doc's the closest thing to family I have left. He gets this serious look on his face. "Let's talk results."

Now I'm starting to wish Mel was with me. "You put me through every scan and test known to medicine. What's the verdict?"

"You're completely healthy, physically speaking—for now. No one can predict how many years you peeled off your liver and other organs. You poisoned your system quite thoroughly taking all those painkillers that contained extra-strength Tylenol. And they did note some unusual activity during the brain scan."

I look him straight in the eyes, soft brown eyes that have a bedside manner all their own. Looking at Doc, I've seen this before. Those brown eyes are concerned, and now, so am I.

"I want to send you to a friend of mine I went to med school with. Her name is Dr. Hawkins. She was a child prodigy and has a doctorate in psychology. And to tell you the truth, I'm not sure if your problems are behavioral," Doc hesitates, "or mental illness. With your history, and the symptoms you've described, it's hard to differentiate. Sadie is intrigued by the unusual brain activity and how it might be related to the problems."

Great, what happens if it is mental illness? Where does that leave me?

CHAPTER 8

Somewhere on the outskirts of Siam sits an old wooden cabin. From the outside, it looks abandoned, left to become one with the woods. The forest, beginning its own reclamation project, pushes weeds through the front porch. A tree has burst apart the rotten wood, thirsting for light, but has found none. Now beaten, its quest denied, the stunted oak has withered. Inside, the darkness has taken over. The blinds are drawn, and a barely visible couch sits in one corner. An early century stove, unused for decades, is the only appliance. Two people converse, one standing, one in a wheelchair.

"I've been waiting several days for you! What took so long?"

"The opportunity finally arose—no need for the attitude. I couldn't believe it when I heard about the accident. What happened?"

"Interference from above and that damn Treadway family."

"I don't understand, Willard. What are you talking about? How are you alive? What am I doing here?"

"It doesn't matter if your dumb ass doesn't understand! You're not here to ask questions. You were called forward to help feed '*the Beast within.*' And what have I told you about calling me by my first name!"

"I do what I want! You've never been a father to me!"

Willard's body sags into the chair. Face sullen, he drops his gaze to the floor. "I regret so much …"

Her body overflows with emotion. Realizing this is the moment she has been waiting for her whole life, she moves closer.

A hand reaches out. "My daughter. Come to me."

Longing for love and acceptance, she takes his hand and leans in. "Father, I've waited for this moment."

A gentle caress turns violent as Willard latches on!

"UHHGG … let … go … of … my … throat."

He shoves her back. "What I regret is your attitude. You sound just like your mother. Despite all the beatings, she never learned her place. Please don't make me do that again."

Willard rolls his wheelchair over the old creaking wooden floor. He stops and spins around, facing his daughter. "You *will* continue to help me."

"And if I refuse?"

"Then I will find your brother and make him take his rightful place beside me. You think he's safe, but you can't keep him hidden forever. I *will* find him."

Much like an addict himself, Willard seems to have gotten a release from this tirade. Calmly, he continues, "Would you like to hear the story of where *the Beast within* came from?"

"JT! Where you been all week?"

Every time I see Rho it makes me smile. "California. Doc sent me to a new therapist in LA"

Rho crinkles up her cute little nose and furrows her brow. "What haven't you been telling me?"

"Trouble sleeping, some crazy dreams. Nothing serious, no worries."

"I can tell when you're lying to me, JT."

I've known this sweet girl for over 20 years. Her family moved out here when she was 6, right down the road from our ranch. Rho used to help take care of our horses, and she was around a lot. I'm 15 years older, and she can still break me down with a look. Sis has had this "awareness" that is almost indescribable. I remember a time, years ago, when she left us all speechless.

My parents, brother, and I were sitting around our kitchen table. We were having a family debate about the type of wood it was made from.

"Your great-grandfather made this table from a tree he found on the back of the property. He walked for an hour through the woods, said something led him to it. Grandpa Jeremiah had never seen a tree like it in Michigan."

"Dad, I'm telling you, this is oak."

"Jonathan, the lines are all wrong for oak. Its color is too dark."

"I think it's walnut." My mom smiled and looked over to me. "What do you think, Jeremiah?"

Just then Rhona, eight at the time, popped through the door. "You guys talking about the table?"

I laughed. "Yep. What do you think?"

"I think it makes me feel wonderful every time I walk by it." Rho got this brilliant little smile as she ran her hand across the table. "It's made from the Tree of Knowledge."

The four of us were a bit stunned by her response. Finally, with a knowing look on his face, my dad spoke up, "Tree of Knowledge? I think I've heard of that."

I must ask, "Knowledge of what?"

"Good and evil, silly. I have to go now." With that, she hopped out the door and went home.

Rhona's voice snaps me out of my memory. "Let me get you some food, and then you can tell me what's going on. Where's that tall beautiful woman of yours?"

I chuckle on the inside; everyone's tall to Rho. She's only about five four.

"Mel's in the U.P. visiting her family. When I headed to Cal, she thought it would be a good time to go up. Hey, this place is empty. Tell Hal you're taking a break and eat with me."

"I'll listen, Father, if you can keep from choking me."

"We all need to learn lessons." A sick evil grin spread across Willard's face. "I love the smell of pain and misery in the morning, it smells like … death!" Willard throws his head back and laughs with a child's glee. "When the Civil War ended, this country was left with an abundance of pain. Dark energy and emotion hung everywhere. As time went on, the darkness rolled into pockets that influenced men to do wondrously wicked deeds. The darkness fed off the despair and misery from the Native Americans as they were slaughtered by white men. All the anguish and pain was absorbed by the darkness, forming the start of *the Beast within.*"

We have some food, and we talk. Rho has an old soul and these green piercing eyes that look deep inside you. "JT, we haven't had a life chat in months. I'm feeling like you need to spill. Is your anxiety level up? You've been smoking more pot lately."

I laugh. "Rhona, have I ever told you about my barter system?"

Sissy stretches her legs out across the red-cushioned seat, leans against the wall, and smiles. "Lay it on me, J-man."

"Remember when I went into recovery for opiates?"

"How can I forget? Your body was shutting down, and your muscle mass was eaten away."

"Taking 12,000 pills in two years will do that. Doesn't leave much room for food. Prior to this onslaught, I was working out like a maniac. For seven years, I rarely missed a day. It was … well …"

Rho finishes my thought, "An addiction. Obsessive compulsive, like lots of addicts."

"In this case, it may have saved me. My addiction doctor told me if I hadn't been in such good shape, I never would have survived as long as I did."

Sissy, nodding in agreement, starts laughing. "Now, is there a point to this, or are you going to keep stalling. What's up with the barter system?"

Rho flashes me "the look" while popping her right eyebrow up, and I bust out laughing. "Wow, little miss smart-ass, you've been practicing in the mirror!"

Sis, unable to hide her smile, softens her eyes. "Learned from the best. Please, carry on."

"After eighteen months of sobriety, I found myself in a worse place than ever before. I was amid a major depression."

"I remember. You rarely got off your couch for a year. We were all scared. Remember that night I had a horrible dream and came by your apartment at, what, 5 a.m.? When I saw the handgun on your kitchen table, I was freaked."

"Not a night I like to think about. I was so lonely and isolated. For some reason, I couldn't pull the trigger. It was then I realized something had to change. Eighteen months sober was the longest stretch I had gone since I was twelve years old. I believe in a reward system for good behavior. For giving up alcohol, coke, and pills of all sorts, I gave myself back something. I took back weed. As soon as I got high, that feeling of loneliness went away. I got active and rejoined life. I went back to work and felt productive again. That's how my barter system started, and I learned to settle."

Or maybe I'm just weak and took the path of least resistance.

Willard continues his tale ...

"*The Beast within* was just getting started. It grew exponentially during times of war. Emotional pain is its forte. After Jeremiah Treadway stood up to my great-grandfather, Basthwine Tithe, *the Beast within* was called upon. The Little's revenge started 84 years ago with the death of Jeremiah Archibald Treadway's youngest child." Willard pauses, basking in the thought of the harvest of innocent souls. "My great-grandfather learned to use *the Beast within* and formed an alliance. He passed this pact down through the generations to me. *The Beast within* has been around during this country's darkest times. After the towers went down, it found its best opportunity yet ... ADDICTION."

Inevitably, the talk turns to the accident. "Can you believe what happened to Willard?"

"To tell you the truth, Rho, I haven't given it much thought."

My eyes wander around the diner. This woman knows I'm tap dancing, as it's pretty much all I've thought about.

"JT, 20 years and you haven't learned yet?" She reaches across the table and takes my hand in hers. "I look up to you. You're like my older brother. We're family. If you hurt ... I hurt." Her touch is reassuring, and her voice is soothing. Once again, she's reaching into my deepest, most protected thoughts.

"I was there. I could feel the presence of 'diabolical influence.' He gave you the 'eight syllables of evil' stare back. My insides were on fire at that moment."

I didn't even broach the subject of Willard with Dr. Hawkins, and I'm not liking what Sis is picking up on. Right now, just thinking about Willard is giving me heartburn.

"JT, that man is as evil as it gets. Something happened in this diner between you two, and it hit me flush!" Rho stops, closes her eyes, and takes a deep breath. She lets it go real slow. "Sometimes I've gotta clear myself, just stop and let all the emotion flow away."

"I'm going to go up and get us both some more coffee, Sis. You sit and relax."

"We're not done here, JT. Don't think for a minute I'm lettin' this go." Rho laughs as I get up. "The antacid's under the front counter."

"Thank—what? How did—" I bust out laughing, shake my head, and stroll to the front.

"Will—er—Father, that doesn't even make sense. What are you telling me?"

"When troops were sent to Afghanistan, *the Beast within* was there to influence certain decisions. The White House was warned about civilian casualties that would result from our invasion—American civilian casualties! They were told this would open a pipeline of heroin directly into our country. The White House was told we needed extra security and extensive checks of all air and sea transports coming from that region of the world. The White House's official response: Our government thrives on death. We are prepared to take civilian casualties. We are fully aware of the pain, misery, and death that will ensue. We just don't care!"

Willard, like a child on Christmas morning, squeals with delight. "And now there's a massive heroin epidemic all the way from the Eastern Seaboard through the Midwest, and fully into rural America! Yesss! Think of it! Heroin leads to death with all that dark emotion in between. Tens of thousands of Americans are dying, and our wonderful government loves it! And the sweetest part … *the Beast within* gorges and grows in strength."

I set the coffee down on the table, "Got a new tat while I was in LA. Want to see it?" I pull my shirt back to expose the tattoo.

"What is it with you and religious icons?"

On the upper middle of my back is a tat of St. Michael the archangel, my protector. On my chest is a crucifix. And now I've got a new tattoo on the back of my right shoulder.

"Why don't you just go to church instead?" Rho loves to give me a hard time.

"I go to church, sort of. Don't funerals and weddings count?"

I'm getting that crinkle and furrow again, with a big smile. "Damn, JT, these angels look great. But what kind of angels carry weapons?"

"Those are swords and battle axes. If you looked closely, you could tell." Now I'm smiling.

She laughs. "Bite me. The one in the middle has a flail. Nice touch. But the writing doesn't make any sense. I count eleven angels, but it says, 'We are twelve.'"

"I'm not quite sure. It just came to me."

I turn and see something in Rho's face—concern. There's more, though it's hidden away and I can't break through it. "What do you know, Sis? What aren't you telling me?"

"You know me. I get these weird pictures in my head. Nothing to worry about."

CHAPTER 9

"What are you going to do next? What am I supposed to do?"
"You screwed up the fire at the diner. You couldn't even keep Jeremiah occupied for more than a month. Just go back and act like the whiny ass bitch that you are." Willard laughs like a sick, deranged drug company CEO. "Just pretend like nothing has happened. Fool the people around you. Make them think you're always there to help."

"What do you mean? What am I doing here anyway?"

"You are serving a purpose—that's all you need to know. Besides, your services may not be needed after today, and you can leave Siam forever. *The Beast within* has something special planned for JT."

Walking out to my jeep, I can't get Willard outta my head. Gotta dull the pain. Time to go home and do the burn. Need to get away! My leg starts jumping, like when I ran out of Suboxone. Got that damn itch in my collarbone. Keep seeing Willard's eyes rolling back into his head.

Brrr! Chillin' is one thing, but it's getting kinda cold out. I swear it was 80 degrees about 5 seconds ago! Man, I'm getting all tit-nipped. But wait, that aroma … that sweet smell … it's not weed, no way. Haven't smelled this in years ... sickly sweet perfumy ... it can't be! I can almost taste it.

My brain is forcing me in that direction.

"Stonow ys stp!"

What? Please, please don't start with the voices.

Before I get to the jeep, I see some kind of huge worm or insect wriggling around in oil on the ground. My knees lock up, and I quickstep it back. Damn, what is that? A three-inch-long black maggot? It's about the grossest thing I've ever seen!

A dark shadow rolls out around the side of a van right in front of me, and my body is slammed by static. What is that smell? Sulfur? Instantly, I'm taken to a turn in the trail. I'm in the woods, breathing hard like I've been walking uphill for an hour. It's so cold, plumes of my breath billow out, freeze in midair, and shatter on the trail. With every step, the crunch of leaves under my feet sends an ice-cold shock up my legs. I'm shaking so hard, I'm forced to stop. Getting that old feeling again, that horrid sense of being lost in life. My mind is hollowed out like a rotted log. My skin—it's peeling, crawling. Not again, never, OH GOD!

I hit the ground in the fetal position and look up to see a giant shadow. It's standing over a fresh kill, legs coiled, letting out a deep, reverberating, bone-crumbling growl! All I can see is a hollow blackness where its eyes should be. I get hit with a wave of stench that almost pulls me back on my feet. I feel like I'm crawling out of my skin and into death.

God help me! I can't live like this anymore! *Take me now!* Ten tons of negativity are assjamming into my brain. The pile of flesh this creature is standing over is oozing closer. That's not flesh. Black, undulating maggots! My heart's in and out of flux, like a flickering light switch.

Can't take a breath, edges are closing in ... vision's ... turning dark ... and gray ...

"Jeremiah."

What just happened? I'm floating away. Afraid to look. Has God finally listened? I've been waiting for the pain to end since He took my family. It's the kind of pain that gnaws away at your soul, pill by pill. Mental illness? Is that what life crapping all over you is? I'm haunted. I'm scared. Is this the end?

"Jeremiah, come back. Open your eyes."

I know that voice. It's so familiar.

When I was nineteen, we had a pile of Valium. Over the course of four hours, I took twenty-four little yellow pills. I was gulping them down—three and four at a time—laughing. About the six-hour mark, I stopped moving. I remember looking down. I was floating above everyone. I didn't know I'd stopped breathing. Addiction plays dirty. It knows you, knows what it wants, and does anything to get it. TAKE CARE OF ME, AND I WILL TAKE CARE OF YOU. I heard someone say, "Jeremiah, come back. Open your eyes." I lurched my body out of the chair and fell on all fours. I crawled to my room and didn't budge for another 24 hours.

My body's coming back ... to life? Once again, I'm on all fours.

Arms wrap around my body. My ass is on the gravel, and I'm propped up against a car. If this is the afterlife, we're all in trouble.

My eyes open slowly, and my vision is hazy. There's a stranger crouched on one knee with his hand on my shoulder. His dark complexion, that accent ... trying to place an origin. He has soft blue eyes, a Mediterranean blue the likes of which I've never seen. Maybe this is Limbo, the place where outcast souls go to haunt the living. That would be okay, I guess. There's a few people I'd love to go eff with.

"It's good to see that you are back with the living, Jeremiah." He laughs. "My name is D'Angelo. Michael Archer D'Angelo."

This guy's seen too many Bond movies. "How the hell do you know my name?"

Just then Rhona comes running like a banshee.

"JT!"

Wow, she's moving. "JT, what happened? I felt your life slipping away!" Tears are streaming down her face.

"Really, not quite sure." I pause for a second, not even knowing what to say. "I think I fainted, that's all. It's no big deal." Like she's going for that. "But this guy here, Michael, sat me up and talked me back."

I'm seeing that look now, the one Mel's been giving me. It's more than disbelief, it's more than concern. It's more like, "Are you crazy?"

"Please don't look at me like that, Sis, he's right—" I turn, and no one's there.

Somewhere in the Middle East ...

"Your mind appears to be elsewhere, as that was not the smartest move on the board."

"I'm sorry, Father, with so many souls suffering —"

"So many souls, Michael, and you can't get your mind off one?"

"This is never a fair conversation." Michael laughs. "You know I'm thinking about Jeremiah."

"You were tasked with keeping him alive, and you've done a miraculous job. If you weren't a saint already, I'd promote you myself." A warm, knowing smile forms. "You are worried about Jeremiah's fate?"

"I am worried about the evil that is seeking him out. Lucifer has a unique weapon in *the Beast within*. The ability to bring about withdrawal is diabolical. Is Willard gaining the upper hand?"

"There are many influences on fate, Michael. You know that. The darkness always has an opportunity, but Jeremiah must continue to fight. He must realize, on his own, that it is okay to ask for help. He must count on others and use their strength to bolster his. We have put elements in place to help him and keep the balance intact. For now, please continue to watch over Jeremiah, as he will need you again. One more thing ..."

"Yes, my Father?"

He roars a wondrous, thundering laugh. "You left your king exposed. Checkmate!"

Shaking his head, Michael looks away and smiles. "Been playing for thousands of years, and I haven't beat Him yet."

CHAPTER 10

"Rho, I appreciate you coming to the station with me. I'm a little scared. Cappy hasn't called me down there since …"

"I know, JT. You don't have to say it."

"I really do. Cappy hasn't done that since my parents and brother were killed in the fire."

"We've never talked about the accident."

"It's been three years, and I haven't talked to anyone about it." The memories of that night start inching back in. "Of course, I was at the bar partying, having a good time."

"I know you feel responsible, but that's just guilt playing with your mind." Rho treads lightly, softening her voice. "It wasn't your fault."

The thread of bewilderment starts weaving its way into my head, then knits frustration, finally creating anger. "Guilt doesn't play with your mind, it smothers you like a 500-lb. bastard and drives you headfirst into life's shitpile!"

The blare of a car horn shakes me out of my head.

"JT! Move back into your lane!"

Swinging back, I pull over on the shoulder. "Damn. Sorry, Rho."

Once you've experienced dark, crippling emotion, it becomes part of your muscle memory. So easy to slide back in, and it seems I've arrived again. "God didn't seem to care that I lost my mind. I couldn't snort enough coke or drink enough liquor to make it go away. The pills just piled misery on top." Zero to depression in less than six seconds, new personal best.

"Jeremiah, life can get crazy, but God does care."

"I believe in God. I believe in the Light. But don't give me that crap about how God never gives us more than we can handle."

"JT." Rho's taken aback. "That's not what I said."

Anger starts pushing its way through. "Pure bullshit. Just ask all the good people who have committed suicide! Seems He gave them too much to handle, gave Dave too much."

"Jeremiah, I'm not the enemy."

Guilt sticks its blade into my gut. "Why am I still here?" Then it starts twisting. "I don't deserve to live."

"JT, let me help. I feel your pain. I will always be there for you." As she speaks, I feel a sense of calm. Sis lays her hand on my shoulder, and it places a smile on my face. Just knowing someone is listening can help.

We roll down the road, and I'm lost in my head again. Samari told me the barn was totally engulfed, smoke billowing out the windows with flames dancing all around. How does a trained firefighter go running into a blaze with no equipment? Jonathan Treadway, my big brother, six years older. All I ever wanted was to be like him. John ran into the barn to save our parents, and he never made it out.

I pull into the police station and throw the jeep in park. Staring straight ahead, I can feel the tears welling up.

"Jeremiah." Rho snaps open her buckle.

My hand goes to my chest. "I've got that flutter thing going on, like my very own mini heart attack."

Emotion and stress pile on. Sickening memories take over. "My heart woke me every morning when I was hooked on opiates." The unrelenting feeling of loneliness is creeping in.

She reaches over and hugs me. Her touch is warm as the sun, and her voice is reassuring. I'm breathing better, and my anxiety is subsiding. "You're amazing, Sis. Let's go in. I'm ready."

"I see you still have your manners."

"Always hold the door for the lady—that's what my dad taught me and my brother. Women are to be cherished and respected." Rhona's arm is looped through mine, and it's giving me strength. But still …

"JT, why did you stop?"

"This weight," I look around, "pulling on my shoulders."

"Bwrestastrng jtjt"

What was that? The voices! Haven't heard them in a couple weeks. I can't even make out what they're saying most of the time. Seems if I smoke enough weed, I don't hear them at all. And lately I've been burning nonstop. Do a wake 'n' bake and don't stop until I hit the pillow at night.

Now I don't want to be here. Maybe we should turn around and leave.

"JT, snap out of it," Rho's whispering. "Get hold of yourself." Sis holds on tighter, and I feel comfort wash through me like the tide.

We walk into the lobby, and Cap is there waiting. "JT, thanks for coming. Always good to see you, Rhona."

I look over to the right, and Doc is sitting there. "What's going on? Why are you here?"

"I asked Doc to join us. What I'm going to tell you is disconcerting at best."

There's no smile on Doc's face today. Those soft brown eyes are looking deep into me. He's got this pained expression, like he's eaten poison and it's twisting his gut into knots. I'm drifting, starting to get that sense of the adhesive losing its hold. Rho senses this and guides me to a chair.

She sits next to me and whispers in my ear, *"Hear us—we will help you."*

My body goes stiff, eyes wide in horror. I spring straight up so fast the chair goes flying backward.

"What?"

Feels like my brain is oozing out my ears. "What did you just say!"

I've lost all sense of perception, seeing my brain in that frying pan. I need to scream! I want to get up, run out the door, and get as far away as I possibly can. I know how to do that.

Doc jumps up. Sissy grabs my arm and sits me back down.

"Easy, JT, easy. Please sit down and calm yourself. I said to hear this out. I will help you." Rhona's whispering now so only I can hear her. "Your brother comes to me in my dreams, so do the others. They tried warning you when we came in."

Doc Riley's giving me that sideways look and rubbing his forehead.

"Haven't taken anything, Doc, not for a long time. Haven't even smoked any weed yet today."

Doesn't mean I'm not thinking about it. Taking a walk in traffic may be the way to go. That's my own police code for doing something hard for escape purposes. Hard meaning liquor, powder, or pills. Maybe even a combo pack special. For me, to jump back into that life would be akin to taking a walk in traffic. It would be exciting for a while, then I would end up getting splattered by a bus.

The look on Cappy's face is priceless. I almost want to laugh out loud, but I'm used to this, used to me.

"JT." Doc's done with the ciphering. "Snap out of your head!"

"Don't think I can do this." Flight takes over. "I just can't!"

I jump up and dip out the door. Standing in the parking lot, I pull that bad boy out and fire it up! I give it a big pull and feel that wonderful smoke filling my head. What was I thinking, going in there straight? Have to get my mind right. I'll go back in when I'm ready. Another pull and I'm on my way, to another, and another … like I said … I'll go back in when I'm ready.

CHAPTER 11

As I walk back in, Rho comes up and gives me a hug. "I told you he'd be back." She's laughing, as the aroma is hanging all over me. "Feeling better?"

Better? Hah, just burned half a Romulan Diesel. Better is a relative term. Crispy is more appropriate.

"Let's do this. I'm ready."

Doc's got a shit-eating grin going, but Cappy's throwing darts my way. "Dammit, JT, I can't have you smoking weed in front of my station."

Sometimes Doc likes to stir the pot. "He's legal, Eugene." He knows Cap's about to lose a nut.

I'm a bit of a stirrer too. "I wasn't in front. I stood out of camera range, in back. Sammy calls it the safe zone."

Seeing a vein pop in Cap's neck always makes me laugh, to myself. Talk about adrenaline flow, Cappy goes from pale to red to purple in about four seconds. He storms out the lobby, swinging doors flying open, and into the outer offices. "Deputy!"

Duty rosters tacked up on a bulletin board are exposed to a hurricane-like gust. As the doors swing back in, the vacuum pulls dozens of airborne rosters back with it. The exploding paperwork is too much, and the three of us bust out laughing. Cap, his face having returned to its normal color, walks back in. Without losing a beat, he struts through the carnage. "Let's go in my office."

I'm still giggling when we sit down.

Cappy takes front and center. "JT, I'm going to just lay it all out for you, and I hope you can maintain."

This isn't Cappy anymore. He's got that "delivering bad news" posture. I'm listening to Captain Eugene Davis of the Siam Police Department. Feels like the knock at three in the morning, the one that makes your heart sink into the floor.

"After Willard's accident, we had his truck hauled back to impound. My detectives found some evidence that allowed us to get a warrant to search his home. The State Police brought in their forensic team. It took almost two months to get it processed. This isn't television, where you get same-day results. The backlog at the lab is seven weeks."

I'm listening, sort of. "Let me guess, you found Willard's porn stash?" I may start laughing. "What, did he have the stalker starter kit? Duct tape, rope, and binoculars?"

I glance over at Rho, and she's staring right at me, right into my eyes. I feel her reaching deep into my head, trying to tell me—

"JT!"

I snap back and look at Captain Davis.

"Stay with me, JT."

Cappy has the same look as when he told me about Dave's suicide. He found me working at the shelter that day. I scooped up two puppies, sat against the wall, and cried for an hour. They fell asleep in my arms. It was the best therapy session I've ever had.

"The forensic team found duct tape with strands of hair, the follicles still intact. JT ... Jeremiah ... we found DNA evidence. The hairs match your father's."

My head feels like it just settled sideways on my shoulders.

"We found an accelerant that matches what the fire investigators found in the barn. And there's more evidence that is still being processed." A loud hiss is piercing my brain like a train whistle at point-blank range.

Captain Davis continues, "They also found some rope. It's being tested for DNA. We expect it to match your mom's."

My head does a 720 with a half twist. What? Am I being punk'd? Is this an episode of *Bones*? What was in that Rommy D?

My fingers are ice cold, and my body starts shivering. Rho sidles up next to me and wraps her arms around my body. The warmth flows, allowing me to catch my breath. As I process what I just heard, my anger starts to flow, and I regain my focus.

"Are you saying that Willard killed my family?"

"It seems that he was involved. We believe he lured your parents into the barn and rendered them unconscious." Cappy stops. "And Willard may have had an accomplice."

"How long will it take for confirmation on the rope?"

"It'll be another week. We also found old paperwork, deeds, and letters that point to a bad history between your families. This goes all the way back to your great-grandfather."

My forehead is squeezed tight, and my jaw is clenched like a vice. I'm focused on giving pain and meting out justice for my family. My eyes give away my intentions.

"JT, I'm not liking the look on your face. Seen it before on men I've had to arrest for taking the law into their own hands. Yes, they were justified, the same as you, if this was the 1800s."

Captain Davis speaks again. "I have known you for your entire 41 years, was best friends with your parents, but I will arrest you if you interfere!"

"No sweat, Cap, you do your thing. Please keep me in the loop on the remaining evidence."

Tell people what they want to hear so they will leave you alone. Alone to take care of the craving in your brain. I know what I need to do—inflict pain, lots and lots of pain. Karma got it right, he's not brain-dead, my nightmares tell me otherwise. Willard's been taunting me from his wheelchair, and he will pay. "Thanks for being here, Doc. Sissy, let's get out of here."

"Now that they're gone, Jim, gotta tell you, that was not easy. And JT is not in a good place. That man has gone through hell already. This is the last thing he needed to hear. Hopefully he doesn't have a full relapse. The pot is bad enough."

"Eugene, that was the last thing I needed to hear. Pull out that bottle of scotch and pour me a double."

"Best thing I've heard today, Jim. But it's going to take more than a double."

It seems the elder statesmen have their own escape …

"Where do you want to be dropped off, Sissy? I'm going home. Need to soothe my savage beast with music."

Rho laughs. "Music and …"

I chuckle. "Weed, of course."

"You can act however you want in front of them, JT, but I know better. I know what you're thinking. Don't go after Willard without me."

"You seem to know quite a bit. I think it's time for a sit down." Pulling over on the shoulder, I throw the jeep in park. Giving Sissy the crinkle and furrow, I start in, "Some crazy-ass shit just went down. I haven't forgotten what you whispered in my ear. And the voice? Did that come out of you?"

"In the first place, I do not look like that when I look at you!" Unable to hide her grin, she laughs and I join her.

I give Sissy a big hug. "Used to think my family was all gone, but I was wrong. Loneliness is a hard feeling to shake, but I've got more than a lot of people out there. I love you, Rhona Alastrina. Please don't ever give up on me."

"Told you before, and I'll tell you again—NEVER!"

"You do owe me an explanation, Sissy. You're different. Sometimes you absolutely blow my mind."

"I don't know how to explain it. Maybe I'm clairvoyant, maybe empathic. At times, I think I'm crazy. Ever since I was a little girl, I've known and felt things that I can't explain." Rho gives a big sigh. "And I get weird dreams. Usually, I never tell anyone about them. But the dreams with your brother are so real, like I have to give a message to you."

"You also said 'others,' the other ones come to you."

"The others aren't as clear as your brother. He has the strongest voice, but I can almost hear them too. It's so strange, like no other dreams I've ever had. And the voice in the station? That just busted out of me. It felt like a bunch of people all in unison. It must be the 'others' I keep dreaming about."

With everything I have heard lately, this doesn't even seem to register on the strange scale. Where's Nick Groff when I need him? Or Zak Bagans, or Chip. Chip Coffey would be so on top of this! Oh well, got my own problems, and I don't think they can help. I don't even have a K2 meter or a paranormal puck. What would I even do with that stuff? Hey, Willard, come over here and let me check your ass for electromagnetic leakage. Let me take a rem pod and jam it down your throat. Well, that might work. I crack me up, and I can't keep it in.

Now Rho's laughing. "I'm glad you're finding humor in this. I've been thinking I'm going nuts."

"That's a subject I can help you with. You don't even crack the top one thousand. I would know, I'm number two."

"Wow." She laughs. "Do I know number one?"

"Number one?" This instantly throws me back into my head. "Yes, we both do."

Anger starts creeping back in, rolling up slowly like a whisper of irritation that won't leave your ears. It starts rubbing on your brain like fine-grade sandpaper, changing your mood slowly. It picks up steam, chafing away at your moral fiber. It makes you think about inflicting pain in ways that would make anyone else run and hide. It rolls faster and faster and faster! You finally explode, ripping that person to shreds! And then it subsides. Your mind is at peace again, all seems right in the world. Serenity.

"When your mind is focused, you hear us as one."

I'm not freaked by that voice. I think I'm beginning to understand.

"JT, I'm picking up on some crazy vibes. You just heard something in your head, didn't you? I could almost make it out. We need to take time and think this through. I need to do some research. Drop me at the library."

"You're right. I need to go home and chill. Dr. Hawkins was insistent that I learn to meditate, and it's time to try."

Tell them what they want to hear so they will leave you alone, alone to take care of that craving in your brain. Time to break out the Old Testament. Willard will atone for his sins.

Rho's laughing. "Eye for an eye?" She pops her eyebrow. "Drop me in front and try and focus until you get home. I'll come by the ranch later."

"Okay, Sis. Peace out." Damn, what man stands a chance with this lady?

CHAPTER 12

I pull off the main road and cruise up the driveway. My windows are down, and I can hear the loose gravel popping under the tires like Bubble Wrap. Stone Sour's "Through the Glass" is on the radio. Doesn't seem that long ago we had horses galloping around the fenced-in area on the left side of the drive. There were chickens, goats, and even a couple potbellies running about. After the fire, I sold off the horses and gave away the rest to our neighbors. I pull up in front of the house that my great-grandfather built. We kept the home up, refurbished the exterior, and remodeled parts of the interior.

I remember when I was about twelve, I asked my dad one day, "Do you think great-grandpa knows what we've done to his house?"

My dad looked at me with his warm, comforting smile. "He not only knows but is very happy with the care we've given it. He built it for all the generations of our family to live in."

I've often wondered how he knew, but Dad was so sure that I never asked.

I scan the property from right to left. I used to see acres of hope that went on endlessly. The fences are all still up. There's several equipment sheds and a small barn in front, adjacent to the house. Off to the right of the drive is "the abyss," a 2,000-square-foot area of nothing but overturned earth. Not a single blade of grass will take root. Hell, not even weeds grow there. It's where the main barn used to sit. After the fire, I had what was left torn down. My neighbor to the south, Jake, brought his son and some heavy equipment over. I watched it all go, bucket by bucket, into the back of a truck. Hauled it away, along with the memories of my parents, my brother, and my life.

I was ready to write him a check for the work, and Jake walked over to me with that side-tilt strut, always playing up to the moniker. "JT, put that checkbook away. We do for each other around here. Your father and I were neighbors and great friends. You ever need anything, son, just ask." With that, Big Jake sauntered off, leaving me with a tear running down my face.

Damn, three years later, and I've got that tear running down my cheek again. The sky is cloud-covered and gray. It's the kind of Michigan sky usually reserved for mid-November. A northeastern wind howls through me. Chills bump up my skin from wrists to neck. I'm the only one left. Loneliness is creeping back slowly, like a faint whisper in my ear, signaling the end. This place seems so … cold.

Walking up the front steps, standing on the porch, can't help but think about the good times we had here. And the fact that those days are gone. Attaboy, just take a wrecking ball and drive yourself deeper into a hole. I can always count on myself for that. Time for some music. We'll go with "Rise Against" for a while. Gotta lift my spirits, so I spark one up. Music's doing its job, so I close my eyes and let the songs take me over. I close out the world and focus.

Something jars me out of my head, and I open my eyes. It's dark out, must have fallen asleep. Dr. Hawkins said it isn't easy to grasp meditation and that falling asleep is a good first step. Well, I got this down—smoke until you need a nap. Maybe we should try this again. I'm liking meditation. I'll just grab a cup of coffee, and we can start this process over. Snap the music back on, and "Animal I Have Become" starts bangin'. Three Days Grace knows about pain all too well. I turn it up and head to the kitchen. I go for the switch—nothing, no kitchen light. My laptop is on, and the music's still going. Strange. The floodlights are on in the front of the house … and everything just went off.

"What in the hell is going on?" Now I'm talking to myself out loud, something I do frequently. "All I wanted is a damn cup of coffee!" My collarbone is going insane.

"HaHaHaHaHaaa."

I freeze in midstep, electric tingles blowing through my body, agony jumping me from behind. I'm slammed with a wave of hatred as it rolls from my insides out.

"Ha Ha Ha Ha Haaa."

Panic, flight, fight, frozen in fear, all in one. My brain is overwhelmed with crushing, vice-like anguish. What's happening? I want to find a closet and crawl into it, hide away, never come out.

"Jeremiah, you will be mine."

I recognize that laugh, the tone of the voice, the arrogance … it just can't be! But I feel *his* presence. Pop Evil's "Deal with the Devil" comes blasting through the speakers!

As fast and loud as it starts, it stops, leaving dead silence. My adrenaline's screaming through my body, but I just … can't … move! There's a squeak off to the side, wheels rolling across my wood floor.

Then, I hear that arrogance again. *"I can find you anywhere."*

A shadow's in front of me, but the voice is coming from behind! I can't move, don't know how to fight this, so I grab the St. Michael medal around my neck and start rubbing it. Pray! I've got to pray.

"Michael can't help you now. *The Beast within* will take your soul for me!"

71

The shadow, like a wriggling infestation of black maggots, bubbles closer, reaching out with its gleaning evil! The blackness oozes toward me, enveloping, its long claws emerging, glistening without light!

"Noooo!" It's got my shoulder and it's pulling me, shaking me. "No, let me go!"

"JT, I'm here and I've got you!"

Willard's got me, and I'm going to die! "No, I won't go!"

"Jeremiah! Wake up!"

I stop shaking and screaming. Swear that was Rho's voice. My eyes open, and ... it's still light out? "What the—"

"You were having a nightmare."

"Oh, my God, that was so real. How did you get in here, Sissy? Where did you come from?"

"I've been at the library for the last four hours, and your front door was wide open."

"That's not possible, I locked it when I came home. I *always* lock it."

"JT, when I came up the front steps, the door was standing open, and you were sleeping on the couch."

Can't shake my head out of the murk. I need to snap my brain to attention. "Could you be a darling and make us a pot of coffee, please?" No way I'm going in that kitchen right now.

Sis starts laughing. "Wow, Mr. No-one-does-anything-in-my-kitchen-but-me."

"Okay, okay, okay, Miss Bitchjustmakeusapotofcoffee!" Now I'm laughing too.

"AHHHHHHHHH!"

"What?" I leap off the couch and run into the kitchen. "Rhona, what!"

"THAAAT!" She buries her head in my chest, pointing at the counter.

"Whoa!" I pull us both back a few steps and stare. "That's bigger than the one in the parking lot."

"It's black! JT, a black maggot?"

This thing is the size of a giant sea slug. My face is sucking inside of itself, trying to escape. Rhona is digging her nails into me and pushing us further back.

"Do something!"

"Oh, now it's a man's job?! Fuck that, I'd rather sell the house than grab that thing!"

I give a quick look up, shake my head, and grab a jar. "Another test, God?"

With a spatula, I flop the creature into the jar and twist the lid on tight. It starts spraying black slime in the glass!

"Whoa! Hey!"

"Don't drop it!"

This thing is definitely pissed off. Setting the jar back on the counter, I look at Sissy and laugh. "Don't think I need any coffee now. But would you like some eggs, prepared using this spatula?" I crack myself up.

"Sometimes you're not as funny as you think." Rho starts laughing but suddenly stops. "What was your nightmare about?"

Before I can answer, she starts shaking. Drops of sweat are forming on her brow. Her eyes start bouncing and rolling up.

"Sink!"

"What?" I catch her as she starts to collapse.

"Getting sick …" We barely make it to the sink! After about 20 seconds, her retching subsides. "Evil."

"What?"

"That thing is evil. Get rid of it."

"How? Bury it? Burn it? I'm open to suggestions."

"I have an idea, but I can't touch it. Grab the jar and put it on your kitchen table."

My eyes open about ten times wider than normal. "Grab the jar?"

"Time to be a big boy, J-man. I'm being guided to put the jar on the table."

Gawd, I hate maggots, but here goes. I do a quick pick, run, and set. My heart's thumping through my chest as I back off.

The mason jar sits peacefully for about ten seconds. The maggot is not happy. It starts thrashing and doing flips! The glass jar begins to vibrate, sounding like drumsticks on the table!

"Rhona. Rhona! What the hell is going on?"

A glow emits from the table, surrounding the vibrating jar. The writhing maggot starts smoldering. The creature lets go with a piercing squeal.

We both jump back. "Damn, Sissy, that was better than a microwave!"

"Don't freak, but you have to open the lid."

"I'm gonna pretend I didn't hear that."

"Please! You have to!"

I take a deep breath and try to steady myself. My hand is shaking as I grasp the jar. Rho touches my shoulder, and my body settles. Unscrewing the top, I feel pressure from inside! I look over at Rhona, and she nods. "Keep going. It's okay."

"Something's pushing!" Power is building inside the jar. A force bellows out of the jar, almost knocking both of us over. A static charge hits me on top of the head, sizzling down through my feet.

And then … silence. The house is filled with an amazing aroma.

"What's that smell?"

"Rose petals. Isn't it beautiful?"

I give myself the sign of the cross. "What happened just now?"

"We released a soul that had been harvested by evil. They have found the Light."

Rhona turns and glides back into the living room. Jaw on the floor, I'm fixated on Sis. She turns around and laughs. "Quit looking at my butt and check out what I found."

"Butt nothing. I'm trying to figure out where your wings are hidden."

CHAPTER 13

Rho has folders, pictures, and who knows what laid across the coffee table. She has her furrow going, looking hard at a photo. It's a family photograph.

"JT, check out this picture from 1932. It's your great-grandfather, great-grandmother, and their two kids. That's your grandfather on the left and his brother. They were six and four years old, respectively. Shortly after this picture was taken, the tragedies started." Rho stops to collect her thoughts, still lost in the photo. She puts her hand to her mouth. "I just can't stop looking at this pic. There's something in the background, and I can't figure out what it is. I am so drawn to it."

Sissy hands it across the table. "Tell me what you think."

The first thing I notice is how much I look like my great-grandfather. I never met him, but I feel like I've known him my whole life. He was only 54 when he passed in 1959.

"Do you see what I'm talking about?"

I refocus and look some more, this time scanning the background. "Can't see what you're talking about."

"Look to the right of your family, toward the barn. See it now?"

"All I see is a faint shadow next to the window. It looks kinda like a big blob or something—can't quite tell."

"That's what I'm talking about! What's causing the shadow? There's nothing there to cast it!"

"Maybe you are on the list after all, Sissy, because I'm not seeing much." For some reason, this is funny to me.

"I'm learnin' to trust my feelings, and *something's not right*." Wow, never seen Sis this worked up.

"I found some disturbing shit at the library and township hall. You need to start taking this stuff seriously. I'm getting scared!"

I get this sudden rush of seriousness and apprehension all rolled into one. Leaning across the table, I take Rho's hand in mine. "Okay, sweetie, it's going to be okay. Breathe deep. Tell me what you found. It's time I started listening."

Tell them what they want to hear so I can go and roll one up.

"JT, what Captain Davis was telling us—it's all true. Willard's great-grandfather, Basthwine Tithe Little, tried to push your great-grandfather off this property in 1926. I found the court records, witness statements, and news articles the *Siam Ledger* printed. It was a big deal."

Never liked history in school and this isn't much better. Please don't take 30 minutes to tell me a 5-minute story.

"From what I've read, Basthwine was a nasty, bullying, abusive man. He had to move from two counties over after he was run out of Plymouth. Basthwine had a knack for hangin' people that got in his way. He was accused of burning down his neighbor's ranch. This all came out in the trial, your great-grandfather's trial!"

Sounds like this guy was a regular Nazi. Willard must be the acorn that didn't fall far. Can we hurry this up? I need to get high.

"In 1925, your great-grandfather legally purchased the property. Once he built the house and barn, Basthwine wanted to take it from him. Mr. Little rode over with his two cousins and tried forcing your great-grandfather out. He threatened to burn the whole place down! He even threatened your great-grandmother's life!"

Whoa, wait a minute here. I gnash my teeth together, and my jaws lock tight. He what?

"Three days after that, Basthwine physically assaulted your great-grandmother. He cornered her on a side street in town and broke her arm. Told her that was a warning and her husband better give up the ranch."

He ... broke her arm! I don't like bullies. Maybe someone should've killed that asshat.

"Your great-grandfather rode into town and found Basthwine in the saloon. He pulled Basthwine out into the street and beat him within an inch of his life. It seems that Jeremiah Archer Treadway was the first person to ever stand up to that inhuman piece of crap."

Yes! You go, Jeremiah Archer! Just jam your thumbs into his eyes and rip his head in half!

"Basthwine had his cousins lie for him to the sheriff, and Jeremiah was arrested. They tried to alibi Basthwine and called your great-grand-mother a liar. His cousins said they witnessed your great-grandfather jump their cousin from behind. Once the trial started, the Littles found themselves in a heap of trouble. Basthwine's violent history was allowed into evidence. Both cousins were arrested for lying to the sheriff and spent six months in jail. Jeremiah Archer was exonerated and even lauded by the townspeople. It was noted in the court records, immediately after the trial ended, that Basthwine threatened to kill your great-grandfather. Not only that, but he said your family would pay for generations to come."

Son of a bitch, that's harsh. But Basthwine must have rotted away in prison, right? Fast forward to the end, please.

"This isn't the worst of it, JT. I've gone through your family's death records. Including your parents and brother, there are a total of eleven suspicious deaths. It starts in 1932 with your great-uncle. He was only four years old when he died from head trauma. I found an article in the *Ledger*. They found him in the barn, *the barn*! The doctor couldn't tell what the cause was, figured he got kicked in the head by a horse. Your great-grandfather was quoted in the article. He swore that the horses were all out in the pen, fenced in. There was an investigation but nothing ever came of it. The article noted a 'dark rumor' among townsfolk that there was a nefarious air surrounding the death."

Wait, wait, wait. What about asshat? "Sissy, stop. STOP."

Sis plops down in a chair, her 108 lbs making a resounding thud. She pulls her long auburn hair away from her face. "Your great-grandfather would've made William Wallace and the rest of my ancestors very proud." Sissy gives me this big warm smile. It seems it's halftime in this game of serious. "Thanks for stopping me. I was getting my scotch up. I felt your thoughts pounding my brain."

Rho stands and shoots me a grin. "*All* your thoughts, you effin jaghole."

"Oops." I laugh. "Is nothing sacred anymore?" I think I'm blushing.

Still sporting a sly grin, Rho continues, "Jeremiah Archer did quite a number on Basthwine, but in doing so he may have unleashed a monster."

Maybe I should spark up that Nebula stump I left in the ashtray.

"Maybe you should."

"What did you say?"

She leans hard on that Emerald Isle accent and laughs. "Spark that stump up, fooker. Yar goointa need it after I tell you what happened to esshet." We both bust out, laughing hysterically, letting the stress flow out.

I lean over to grab the roach and stop midreach.

I get the look with the brow-pop. "JT, are you showing some restraint?"

I throw down a big sigh. "This is life-and-death shit going on. I think it's time to clear my head. The weed ain't helping."

Sis tilts her head, eyes widening. "Jeremiah's putting on the big-boy pants," she says, laughing. "It's about time."

Before I can give a smart-ass response, Rhona starts back in. The tone of her voice darkens like nightfall. "JT, your great-grandfather really did lay an ass whooping on Basthwine. He put that man in a wheelchair for life. There was a lot of head trauma too. Basthwine Tithe's state of mind was in question after that. He was locked up in Northville State Hospital's criminally insane wing. This goes beyond fate, JT. The past has met the present! You look so much like your great-grandfather it's, it's crazy! I found a picture of Basthwine Tithe, and it might as well be Willard. They look identical!"

Then bring it on. I feel my family, all of them, streaming through my veins. I need to hear what they have to say, so I focus … But, I get nothing.

Rho does a double take and holds the second, fixing her green eyes on mine, a wry grin forming. "You've got a lot to learn, Jeremiah." Sissy continues with the story.

"By the time your great-grandfather died in 1959, there were open whispers about the 'Little Curse.' There have been accidents in and around the barn, probable suicides, heart attacks, some crazy stuff. And then there's," Rhona stops midsentence and shifts her gaze to the floor, "the fire that took your parents and brother."

A thousand images stream through my head, like a slideshow at warp speed. My anger is focused, firing on all cylinders, working itself into a frenzy. I can feel my hands on Willard's throat, choking him so hard they join! I slide them up, one on his chin and the other on the side of his head ... my focus is clear ... my anger channels into one pure thought ... SNAP!

"Focus your thoughts, and we will have vengeance."

I sit in stunned silence. Did I really, truly hear that? Or am I clinically insane? It sounded like multiple people, all at once. It made me feel like I was at the kitchen table with my family, twelve of us, getting ready to break bread.

I never heard my great-grandfather speak, but I'm sure his was one of the voices. My grandfather, my parents, I heard my parents ... and my big bro ... I know that deep resonance in his voice ... *they spoke to me as one.*

Really, JT, really? You are going off the deep end.

I'm afraid to look at Rho. She's probably on the phone ordering me that double sleeve wraparound. But it felt so sweet, so pure, like ... like that knee-high fastball on the inner half of the plate. Just drop the hands and snap the bat through the zone! It's that moment when Louisville meets horsehide. It's such a pure feeling, such a rush that I never thought I could feel again, until now.

I need to look at Rho, wanting some reassurance ... or just a good hug and a ride to the asylum. I slowly, agonizingly, turn my gaze toward Sis. She's got a huge smile going from ear-to-ear. "Chicks dig the long ball, JT." She laughs. "But don't get cocky. Failing 70% of the time might get you in baseball's Hall of Fame, but not life's."

Rho sits up straight and starts getting serious on me again. "Some things come easy to you, but not this! I'm sensing this is a dangerous time for you—there's no control yet. Willard's not going to pipe a fastball, he's coming off-speed, something you're not expecting. You can't be a guess hitter with him. Keep your hands back and adjust to the pitch, maybe even go the other way with it. Stay balanced in your head, Jeremiah. It's a mental game."

"Who have you been channeling, Tony Gwynn? Rod Carew?"

"You have to stay within yourself, stay humble, unselfish, and don't get cocky! We can get through this!"

"Rhona Alastrina Cairstine MacVicar, my li'l Braveheart." I'm laughing. "How does one get two middle names?"

"One has a mother, two grandmothers, and parents who couldn't make up their mind."

"It's a beautiful name, but then again, what's in a name, li'l B?"

"Oh, God, not another name for me." Sis is crackin' up. "How do you keep them straight?"

"One for every deadly sin I've committed."

"I only count six names, but aren't there seven deadlies?"

"Who says I'm done with your nicknames?" I feel serious coming on. "Pretty sure I'll come up with one more by the time I'm done with Willard."

CHAPTER 14

Michael Archer D'Angelo appears from behind the hanging drapes, his wings tucked neatly to his back. "Our Father." Sheepishly he continues, "You called me forth?"

"Yes, Michael, fate is changing circumstances as we speak."

"I could tell You weren't happy, what with the hailstorm. This is about Jeremiah?"

"He doesn't seem to be learning from his past missteps. Jeremiah has made some progress but is still walking his path alone. I have taken great care to place opportunities within his reach. As he continues to take singular responsibility for vengeance, fate is being dictated by Lucifer."

God sighs. "Jeremiah is stubborn. He has not learned to harness his family's power, nor has he fully accepted Rhona's help. His next headbang will be his last. When he goes charging after Willard, Jeremiah will lose his life."

"But, Father, how can you be so sure?" Michael lowers his head, already knowing that was the most ridiculous thing he has uttered in a thousand years.

"You are not to interfere in Jeremiah's life anymore. He must accept the fate he has created for himself."

"What is to become of his soul, my Father?"

"He must hang in Limbo until I decide. I am not angry with Jeremiah, only disappointed." Our Father sees Michael's body sag, looking downtrodden. "You are fond of this one, no?"

"I have put much effort into saving him, as he's only guilty of being human. Is there no room for Jeremiah in Heaven?"

"Michael, you are my truest warrior, having faithfully served me for thousands of years. You know as well as anyone, there must be a balance maintained between good and evil. Right now, Jeremiah falls somewhere in between."

"How ya doing today, JT?"

"I was just thinking about calling you, Sis. Then the phone rang."

"I know. That's why I called." Rho laughs. "I could feel it."

"Was that the craziest thing last night? I've never seen hail that big before."

"I don't know if *crazy* is the right word. I was filled with anxiety and panic. Something's not right."

"Mel called last night when it started. She's due back any time now. I'm missing her a lot. It's been almost a month since I've seen her."

"Well, you two enjoy each other, but be careful. I had a crazy bad dream, and I'm still trying to figure it out. It was trying to give me a message for you. I was in the woods, but it was your kitchen. The letter V? It makes me think Willard is around. Please be on the alert. I can't help but feel something bad is going to happen."

"All right. If I'm getting crazy shit going on, I'll shout. With Mel, I'm thinking it'll be fine tonight."

"Okay, but I'm serious now. Shout loud if you need help. Give your sweetie a big hug for me, and come by the diner for breakfast tomorrow."

"You got it. We'll see you tomorrow."

That's a wee bit disconcerting. Rhona's been spot-on lately. Maybe I'll walk through the house, check the closets, call a paranormal team, smoke a joint. *Bam!* We have a wiener!

No, No, NO. Keep a clear head! God, why do you test me so? Do you still hate me? Haven't I suffered enough?

Dammit, JT, take a deep breath and relax! You know in your heart that God loves you, protects you, has a plan for you! Does God really torment you? Fate can be influenced by that evil bastard, too. Remember, it's only fate if you act on it, good or bad. It's easiest to blame God, yell at him, curse him, challenge him. It's also a big mistake.

I've always felt the demons nipping. They enter your thoughts, alter your actions, and drive a wedge deep into your soul. It comes from down below—Diabolical Influence, the eight syllables of evil.

I hear Mel coming up the drive at cruising speed, engine screaming. "Baby!"

"Mel!"

I give her a great big hug and spin, all in one. "Oh babe, I've missed you."

"Missed you too, JT."

"So, how's your mom and the rest of the family?"

"They're all doing well. How's things here?"

I'm getting that itch again. I hop up and look out the front door. Nothing moving, seems quiet.

"You okay, JT? You seem jumpy."

"I tried calling but couldn't get through. I know coverage sucks up there, so I just waited until you came home. Cappy laid some crazy-ass shit on Rho and me. Totally blew my mind. Baby, he said Willard Little killed my family."

"What! Oh, hell, is he sure?"

"They found evidence at Willard's house that ties him to the deaths. That skank killed my parents and brother. Cappy also believes he had an accomplice."

With that, Mel's expression changes, surprise turning to angst. "What do you mean accomplice?" She almost sounds pissed. "Do they know who?"

"There's more evidence that's being processed. Plus, Rho found a bunch of info on a feud between Willard's family and mine! The newspaper talked about the 'Little Curse' and—"

"What evidence? Are they sure? What do you mean Rho found info? What's she doing sticking her nose into this? That bitch needs to back off!"

I've never seen Mel act like this, and now I'm getting upset. "Rhona has been my rock, you back the hell off her!"

I'm getting that itch again, deep in my collarbone. I start looking around. What the shit's going on?

Mel slides over, puts her arms around me, and gives me a little kiss on my neck.

Can't help but be liking this. "Mmmm, baby, you do know how to make me feel good."

Mel whispers in my ear. "JT, I'm sorry, please sit down. I'm not mad at her, it's just … this is a lot to deal with. Let me make you something to drink. Why don't you get high and tell me everything?"

I watch her from behind as she struts into the kitchen. "Taking a break with the weed. I need to be able to think clearly."

"Oh, babe, do you think that's a good idea?" Mel's sounding disappointed. "It helps with your anxiety and stress."

"Lately, it's become a hindrance. That shit's been slowing me down."

Suddenly, my nose gets this blast of horrid odor, like dank, moldy socks. It can only mean one thing. "Hey, Mel, did you open the valerian tea?"

Mel's laughing. "How did you ever know? I'm going to make you some. It will help you to relax."

Ahh, valerian tea, the plant they derive Valium from. Talk about a chill pill, this stuff rocks. It's got a terrible taste, but the effects are nice. "My cup's hanging under the cupboard."

"Don't worry, I'll add some flavor so it's drinkable."

Maybe the tea will settle my yips. There was a change in Mel's demeanor when I brought up Willard and the evidence. "Maybe I should call Rho."

"Here's your tea, baby. What did you say? Something more about Rhona?"

"Oh, did I say that out loud? Just thinking I should call her."

"Give her the night off. I've got you all to my own now, so drink up and relax."

"Thanks, baby." I take a big sip, and damn, this is bitter. "Thought you were going to add some flavor. What did you cut it with, strychnine?"

She gets this sultry lean. "I added something special, just for you, some Mel luvin. Drink up, baby."

Back in my head. How can I get through to my brother, my family? Where are they when I need them? I take another big sip. Yuck, the tea tastes worse than usual. Meditating would be perfect, except that dumbass me never took it seriously.

I catch myself rubbing my collarbone. I can feel Mel hovering, and it's starting to creep me out. Can't help but feel I should talk to Sis—wait, what did she tell me? Trying to work through the fuzz that's growing in my brain.

I set the cup down. "Oh, my head feels like thick pea soup." My brain's turning into goop.

"Can't keep my eyes open." Feels like I've been bonging weed all day. "This tea is stronger than usual."

I look up, and Mel is pacing back and forth like a tweaker who can't figure out what to do. Her gorgeous blue eyes have darkened at the edges. She's got this look about her, stalking, trying to find a weakness, much like a predator in the woods. I'm trying to talk, but I can't open my mouth, jaws rusted together. I'm losing it … fading off … my eyelids closing like a weighted drape.

CHAPTER 15

"Rhona!"

"Captain Davis. Oh my God, am I glad you're here!"

"Where the hell is JT? I've been calling him for two hours with no response. He's not at home?"

"Cappy, I had the worst feeling. I'm scared. He didn't answer my call, so I came over. There's no one here, and the place looks spotless. I talked to JT this morning. He said Mel was coming back from the U.P. soon. She must have done something. I'm telling you, you have to believe me, I can feel it!"

"You don't have to convince me, Rho. My gut's telling me the same thing. I was calling JT to tell him about the rope we found. The DNA matched his mother's. I'm highly suspicious of Melchiah. We can't find any info on her prior to seven months ago. It's as if she didn't exist. As far as her family goes, living in the Upper Peninsula, it's all fabricated."

"JT met Mel seven months ago, and they've been together ever since. He fell hard for her, like he was put under a spell. JT was so happy I ignored my senses, put them aside. You need to hear what I dug up on JT's family history."

Rho spills out everything she found. Arms folded tight, one hand rubbing his chin, Captain Davis takes it all in.

"I know about all of this. JT's dad and I talked about it many times. We kept it from Jeremiah on purpose. We wanted the tale of the curse to end, figuring the more it was talked about, the more it would be kept alive. JT's grandfather, Jonathan, was 80 years old when he passed in 2006. From the outside looking in, it was a heart attack. JT's dad found his father dead in the barn. Doc kept it wrapped tight, listing heart failure on the death certificate. But I've got to tell you, Rho, it was anything but natural causes. He died with such a look of horror on his face it would make Stephen King proud. The funeral home director tried for three days to change his face to a peaceful look. Every night it was fixed, and the next morning it would be back to that look of horror. Finally, JT's parents had him cremated. They refused to bury Jonathan with that image still there. After ten years, I still consider this an open case. JT's grandfather was in perfect health."

Rho is crying now, unable to listen anymore. Cappy moves close and gives her a hug. "Sweetie, there's more, and it has to do with you."

Snapping back to reality, she fixes her gaze straight ahead. "I know what you're about to say. I felt it back then."

"The fire at the diner?"

"Yes. I know it was meant for me. I was supposed to die there. The curse tried surrounding and suffocating me. A hand pulled me up. I crawled across the floor following a dim light. A pair of wings led me through the smoke. When the EMTs found me, I was passed out behind the diner."

Cap gives himself the sign of the cross and appears lost in thought for a moment. Rhona busts out a smile. "Aww, that was really sweet, Eugene."

"What do you mean?"

"Thanking God for bringing me to Siam and watching over me. That was nice."

Stunned, he laughs. "I kinda feel sorry for whoever ends up married to you."

Captain Davis's face grows serious again. "We worked that crime scene for weeks. I went side by side with the fire investigators, sifting through the ash. Every intuition I had told me Hal did not burn his own place down. That man loved the diner just the way it was."

Am I alive? Do I dare open my eyes? My head feels trampled by a thousand tanks. Am I back in detox? I don't remember ordering my wrists seared to a medium rare. I'm tied off and hanging from a beam, punished by gravity. Got a sharp pain in my stomach, reminiscent of tainted acid from days gone by. What the hell happened?

Try and remember ... *think* ... I was with Mel ... the tea ... everything went fuzzy ... Damn, is Mel Willard's accomplice?

No, no, no effin way!

Okay, Gumby, you're in denial because that bitch put a whoopin on your ass.

How could I be so stupid? She made me feel good, like a drug I couldn't live without. How can someone smart be so foolish? It's the story of my life!

"Jeremiah, open your eyes."

I know that voice, the accent ... slowly, I peek.

"You must listen to me, Jeremiah. You are in great danger."

"Michael! Thank God you're here. Cut me loose!"

"Stop and listen! I cannot free you. God won't let me interfere anymore. You must focus."

"What? What do you mean God won't let you interfere?"

"JEREMIAH! They will be back to exact their sick vengeance. You are to be tortured and killed. Your fateful lives are extinguished. I cannot save you again."

"Save me again? What the hell are you talking about?"

"Hell is on its way, Jeremiah! The air is thick with the Evil One's presence. Lucifer has taken humanity's darkest emotions and formed the demon known as *the Beast within*. Willard and the demon conjured Melchiah from the slime of the forest. You must focus on Rhona Alastrina. Calm your thoughts and reach out to her. I am in a bit of trouble with our Father, so I must go now. For once in your life, Jeremiah, listen to me!"

"Michael, what in God's name are you talking about? Will you please cut me down? Michael?"

Sonofabitch, he's gone! How does he *do* that?

Maybe you're just hallucinating like a mofo. Maybe he doesn't exist. I mean, this is just crazy.

Too much acid, JT, too much of everything. Who could have figured four for the fourth was over the top? Maybe my brain flipped and there's no going back.

But I've felt a presence my whole life. Maybe he does exist …

The Beast within? Lucifer? Holy crap!

Mel? Conjured from slime? What?

Stand up fool, relieve the pain, stand up!

I push, but my legs are dead, and I slump back down. Rho, focus on Rho, empty your mind, focus! Rhona … help … help me …

"Rho, sweetie, are you okay?" Cappy catches her as she falls to one knee. "What are you picking up on?"

"My legs went numb, my wrists are burning, and I've got a sharp pain in my stomach. Cappy, we need to get into your car. I need to follow this. We can find JT, but I can't walk."

"I'll carry you to the car. Let's go!"

CHAPTER 16

The bright sun cannot penetrate the dark evil that envelops the old cabin. Dead vines crawl from the woods, their rotting leaves wrapping the exterior with the stench of black slime. Inside, two creatures converse; one is standing and one sitting in a wheelchair.

"Willard, we need to get rid of JT. Let's go end it ... now!"

"It's time for you to disappear. That pain in the ass, Michael, has interfered again. He has been a problem for us. Jeremiah Treadway will be ours. Let him feel safe for now. We will prey on his weaknesses, *the Beast within* will see to it. After today, Jeremiah is on his own. Michael will be gone; *the Beast* has foreseen it. We will take his soul very soon for our own devices. If you are needed again, *the Beast* will bring you forth."

"I'm not going anywhere, Willard."

"Don't defy me! I do not like that tone!"

"I don't answer to you, Little!"

"My name is Willard Basthwine Tithe Little, and you *do* answer to me! I was named after my great-grandfather and handed the reins of the curse. *The Beast within* brought you forth from the slime in the woods. He will send you back for your insolence if this continues!"

"I want a piece of that little bitch, Rhona! Then I'll take care of JT myself!"

"You will do as you are told! Melchiah, my dear Melchiah Immerson, you were created and so named to influence and undermine Jeremiah. You have kept him in a prison of sorts until we were ready. Jeremiah will be released after one day, as it was in the Bible. You do not understand, as you were created with a darkness and no soul. Basically, bitch, you are not real."

"The hell I'm not! I feel life!"

"You feel what we let you feel! Greed, lust, envy … that is what you feel. Jeremiah was recovering and learning to be humble, of service to others, and his faith in God had come back. You fed his addictive thinking, and that was the in we needed. For your efforts, I will give you Rhona. Use your jealousy and turn it into wrath. She will be our biggest obstacle, but it won't be easy for you."

"Hah! I'll eat that bitch for lunch!"

"She is so named by God! Rhona Alastrina Cairstine MacVicar was plucked by fate and delivered to Siam. God is devious when it comes to dealing with evil. He believes in balance and knew she would be needed. He's quite adept at countering our moves, that's why he's God. Rhona is more powerful than she knows. *The Beast within* will be there to cloud her mind, allowing the deception to occur. You and my daughter will end Rhona's life. But remember, Jeremiah Treadway is mine."

With a slight toss of her head, Mel flips her hair back. As she sits, a jackal-like grin forms. "How would you like her to be found?"

"Oh, my dear Melchiah, I have the perfect way to make a statement. This death needs to be rubbed in God's face! What do you think of this …?"

CHAPTER 17

"Where are we heading, Rho?"

"North, just head north. I'll tell you when to turn."

"Talk to me, sweetie, what are you feeling?"

"JT's in a lot of pain, but the danger doesn't seem imminent anymore. I smell something old and musty. Jeremiah knows where he is. Turn off the road in a bit—it's getting close."

"There's a two-track up here that heads all the way to the back of the property. I've chased JT around these woods before. That kid was so high on acid one night, it scared the hell out of me. About 20 years ago, on the Fourth of July, he and his crazy-ass friends were being stupid. He almost died that night. Did JT ever tell you about that?"

"No." She laughs. "We had just moved here, and I was only six, but I'll never forget—it was my first fireworks. Right before it started, my dad was up and yelling, 'There's two people walking right through the launch zone. Stop!' I tugged on his shirt and told him not to worry—that it was JT, and he'd be okay."

Cappy rubs his forehead and chuckles. "Those two idiots were so high. They walked through the edge of the crowd and cut across the open field. It was turning dusk, so the techno people were sending up testers. We were yelling and waving at JT and his buddy Joe, but they just kept on walking, oblivious to it all. I thought one of the rockets got launched right up their ass. They got to the other side of the open field, realized what they had done, and ducked out into the crowd. As soon as the show ended, I went looking for those two. Joe was laying on the ground, staring up at the stars. But JT, that cocky shit, was across the parking lot, laughing his ass off. He was pointing at me and my deputies, laughing, calling us the Three Stooges. He started yelling, 'Here I am, Moe,' like it's the funniest thing he ever heard. Soon as I locked gaze, he bolted. I chased him on foot for over an hour. He led me up through here toward the family hunting cabin."

All the blood's run out of my arms, and my body has gone numb. Is this the end? When they find me, I'll be a skeleton, my eyes and flesh picked clean by crows. Then what? How will I be judged? Will Michael be there to say I told you so? Will I feel God's wrath?

No matter what, I'm sure the pain will be gone. That's something. I've always wanted the pain to stop. Prayed for God to take my life, and now it's happening. Such a wasted life, and no one cares. The cold is wrapping itself around me. Looking for the Light, but I get nothing but gray …

"JT."

"Jeremiah."

This is better, no gravel up my ass. But I'm not really floating, just kinda laying down. Arms feel better, though. Wait, wait, wait, I can feel my arms? There's something stuck in one of them …

"Jeremiah, open your eyes."

Oh, I'm not falling for this again, but that's not Michael's voice. It sounds like Doc. All this time and I didn't know Doc was Him? I guess God would enjoy a good twelve-year-old scotch. Nooo, it's got to be wine. All they would need is water. God calls out, "Son, come over here and make us a good Chardonnay" … well, probably something red—

"JT, snap out of your head!"

Whoa, okay, that was definitely Doc. Opening my eyes, I realize I'm not dead. Kind of a bummer—I was looking forward to a good glass of wine. Rho and Cappy are standing behind Doc. All three are busting out smiles like I've never seen. "Don't have to ask where I'm at. Must be happy hour, the way y'all look."

Doc laughs. "You're in ICU. Didn't know if you'd make it."

"Hope there's something good in that IV. Hate to waste a vein."

Sissy hops over. "Always the smart-ass, JT."

She hugs me with all the warmth of the Son. Pretty sure God knows I don't really want to die. I'm just not sure how to live.

"You were dehydrated, JT, that's a saline solution, nothing more." Doc continues, "If these two hadn't found you, we wouldn't be having this conversation."

Cappy steps around and has a seat. "Mel drugged you. Preliminary tests show—"

"Rat poison?"

Cappy gets this twist to his face. "How did you know that?"

"You don't want to know. Let's just say I'm a professional drug taker."

Doc interjects, "It wasn't enough to immediately cause death, but it put you down long enough for them to kidnap you. It's working its way out of your system, and we've given you something to move it along. You'll have to stay in the hospital overnight."

Just effin great. All I want to do is chill to some music.

Cappy stands up. "I'll be back tomorrow, JT. You rest for now. I'm going to need your statement in the morning. We've got an APB out for Willard and Mel. I've got several deputies staking out the hospital in case those two make another move. You'll be safe."

"I'm going to stay with JT. I'll keep him company." Sissy leans over and whispers, "I grabbed some weed for you."

That gets me smiling, except I know better. "You're not the only one studying behavior. That smirk is your tell."

Sis is a bit on her heels. "Oh, really?"

"You're bluffing, bitch." I chuckle. "And I'm staying clean, at least for a while."

"You passed my test, J-man. And don't call me a bitch, effstick." Rho starts giggling, and it's contagious. Even Doc catches it.

Cappy's busting out a smile, "Okay, children—all three of you—behave, and I'll see you all tomorrow."

Doc rolls the squeaky-ass physicians' stool over and takes a seat. "Jeremiah, did I hear correctly?"

I laugh. "I don't know, Doc. Is your hearing aid turned up?"

Doc Riley looks left, looks right, and flips me off, flashing a big smile.

"I guess that means it's working." The three of us bust out laughing.

"Yes, Doc, I'm clearing out the cobwebs. But it's only been a couple days, so hold the applause."

"Jeremiah, I will always applaud a good decision. Stay with it."

Sissy drags her chair in closer. "JT, you once told me that getting clean was the hardest thing you had ever done. Until you tried staying clean."

I can feel my temperature rising. "Your brain doesn't just shut itself off. Addictive thinking permeates every facet of your life, it influences everything you do." Frustration, it seems, never wanders too far off. "That's the magic trick no one has solved!"

How do you turn it off?

CHAPTER 18

Never thought I would be so happy to see my house.

"I've got to pick up a shift at the diner, but I'll bring you some food when I get off."

"Thanks for everything, Sis. It meant a lot for you to stay the night with me. Hospitals creep me out. Please, keep your head on a swivel. This whole situation has been wild."

"What else, JT? I can feel your apprehension. What's going on?"

"I don't quite know. My collarbone's been going nuts since we left the hospital. When that happens, something bad always follows. Maybe you shouldn't go to work."

"I'll be fine. Tracey called and they need some help. How about if I call you on my break?"

"It's Sunday, Sis. Hal closes at 2 p.m. on the weekends."

"They have a group of 30 people that asked Hal to stay open for them. It's some church group, and you know Hal, he always accommodates this town."

"Sounds good. I'm going in and kicking back. Got my slugger sitting by the couch, just in case."

When Rhona arrives at the diner, Tracey's car is the only one in the parking lot. The skies have gone from clear blue to cold and gray. As she exits the car, her body shimmies from her heels to her head. "Brrrr, I swear it was 80 degrees about 5 seconds ago."

I don't know if I can just sit here and do nothing. I've got a running loop going through my head. Over and over, I'm dismantling Willard, body part by body part. *Take care of me and I will take care of you.* My pleasure center is starting to take over, giving me these thoughts, these cravings …

"Michael? You haven't been to the River in over a century." Gabriel laughs heartily. "You're hiding again, aren't you?"

"I have openly disobeyed our Father. How could I have thought He would not know? I am fearful of His wrath."

"Once, long ago, I too was disobedient." Gabriel sits down next to Michael. He gazes across the water into an impenetrable mist on the far bank. "And look what it did for my career."

"I weep for the weary, the suffering masses, unwarranted death by the thousands, and yet my thoughts are of this human. I shed a tear for Jeremiah, but he is only one of many who are caught up in life. Still, this one man can fill me with sorrow."

Gabriel smiles and puts an arm around Michael. "Old friend, He has been calling. No more hiding. You must go see Him."

A glowing warmth encompasses both, causing them to look up.

"I knew where you'd be, Michael." An understanding smile breaks out. "Your heart and soul are in the right place. I will not judge you harshly for that. Humans have perplexed me for centuries. I would not expect otherwise for anyone else."

"My Father, I thought it well to give him another chance. This situation has shaken me, but my faith in You is unwavering."

"Diabolical Influence is bubbling out, Michael. Balance is tilting toward evil as we speak. You will always be, to borrow an expression from the military, our 'Special Ops' Angel. My faith in you is unwavering as well. I may need you to run another mission soon."

"Rhona! Thanks for coming in. Hal's on his way, and I'm going to need some help. The group will be here in about a half hour."

"No sweat, Tracey, I can always use the extra money. What do we have going on?"

"Prep work first. We're all alone until Hal gets here. Let's go in the back."

"Oooh, Trace, what happened?"

Noticing her scarf had dropped slightly, Tracey readjusts. "Oh, that. Just some crazy sex with my boyfriend last night."

"Wow." Rho nervously laughs. "Looks like someone had you in a choke hold."

No matter how hard I try, my focus won't leave Willard. My brain is deadlocked between sword and fists. My head goes Old Testament. I need to beat him, just as my great-grandfather did, with my bare hands.

Thinking about smashing his face, taking out all my frustrations with life, is giving me a rush! I can make myself right, retake control, gain the upper hand …

"Michael, it is almost time. Lucifer is hiding his intentions well. He is trying to divide us, deceive us, but I will not stand for it. Willard and *the Beast within* are getting ready to make their move. It will be soon now."

Rho follows Tracey into the back. "So, Trace, who's the new boyfriend?"

"The marks aren't really from my boyfriend. I got into an argument with my dad." Tracey pauses. "He's a real bastard."

Before Rhona can react, a voice is heard from behind, "Real bastard? That's an understatement."

The hair on Rhona's arms stands straight up, an icy chill blasting up through her spine. She stares at Tracey, eyes pinned wide. How could she have been so stupid? What happened to her senses? Tracey has this look of sorrow, as if she's almost apologetic. A squeal of ecstasy erupts behind Rhona. "Rhona, sweetie, it's time to turn and face your destiny."

She spins to face Mel. "That's right, bitch, it's me, and my friend *the Beast within*." Behind Mel, a dark, smoky shadow drifts up through the ceiling tiles. It leaves a black, oozing maggot in its wake. Mel picks up the little beast. "Glorious little creature, isn't it?" She slowly squeezes her hand until it bursts, slime busting out from between her fingers!

Melchiah slowly licks her palm up through her forefinger. "Mmmm, tasty too. Another soul lost forever." She snaps the residue to the floor and screams with delight. "You haven't been prudent in refining your skills, 'li'l B'!" She continues, mocking, "The Evil altered your senses, allowing you into this situation. Not so special now, are you, JT's 'punk rocker'?"

"I'll punk rocker you, esshet!"

Can't believe I was so blinded by Mel. She always knew what I wanted, yet I never questioned it. My brain kept telling me more—*you need more Mel.*

I will take care of you if you take care of me. I stumbled across that bitch in the woods. That's what I get for wandering too close to Little's property. The trail in the woods! Why didn't I see this before? That's where Willard is! I grab my sword and head out the door … this ends today!

"Events have been set in motion, all is not well. You need to try and persuade Jeremiah to stop. Use whatever truth you must. If he continues down this path he will die … today!"

"As You wish, my Father."

Rhona steps toward Mel. "I've been waiting for this for awhi—" Rho's body hits the floor. Tracey stands behind her, pipe in hand. "Now what do we do with her, Mel?"

Mel cackles like a bitch gone unhinged. "Leave it to me! I have something special in the works." A darkened elemental glow surrounds Melchiah. Her cocoon now shed, she morphs into the next stage of evil. She pulls out a bag and begins taking out its contents, her voice deepening as she speaks. "Help me get her on this table."

Tracey is horrified as she looks at a syringe, spoon, leather strap, and a small packet. "What are you going to do with that stuff?"

"I told you there was something special planned. Your father and I decided some pure Afghani heroin would do the job. We talked about cutting it with some fentanyl, but that would kill her too quickly. We want her to suffer for a while. It's time for Rhona to take the plunge. We're going to send her off on a one-way trip."

Mel's head twists as if hit with a stuttering spasm. Snapping her head back in place, eyes now blackened and hollow, she stares at Tracey. "If you can't handle this get the hell out of here. Otherwise, tie her off. I need a good vein."

Tracey bolts out the door, running without looking back.

"Queasy bitch, must be too much like her mom. Can't wait to rub this in Willard's face." With Melchiah's transformation underway, she loads up the syringe and plans her exit.

CHAPTER 19

My overriding urges to kill that sonofabitch are guiding me. I will fight for you, family. If vengeance is the Lord's, then revenge is mine, all mine! I don't need help from anyone else. I'm strong enough to get this done on my own!

Ohh, JT, this is familiar, think about this. Wouldn't it be better if Sis and Cappy were by your side?

No, this is on me!

Michael said—

Stop! Don't even mention that, whatever he is, thing, guardian, invisible friend. What the hell does he know?

Well, dumbass, he knows you!

He's not here. Michael Archer D'Angelo abandoned me, just like everyone else. Pulling over, I stop.

Breathe, JT, deep breaths, let life come to you for a minute. What's your plan, man?

Hadn't really thought this through. Guess I'll go in and beat him to death.

No, if a car wreck didn't do it, that probably won't cut it.

Cut it? I've got my great-grandfather's sword, given to him by his father. I'm going to lop off Willard's head. I can hear Ernie Harwell's iconic voice …

"*If you're just tuning in, it's been a real barn burner here in Siam. It's the bottom of the ninth, two outs, bases loaded, with the slugging lefty at the plate. Pain is on first, with misery on second, followed by death on third. Little drilled all three hitters just so he could face Treadway. In his last at bat, Jeremiah took a third strike looking, standing there 'like a wraith by the side of the road.' The count's full of death, and the spirits will be rising on the pitch. JT's down three family members, and this is a do-or-die situation! Treadway gets set in the box, hopefully not one made of pine, and digs in. Crouched in his familiar stance, a la Richie Hebner, hands back and sword at the ready.*"

"*Most people don't know, Ernie, that Hebner digs graves in the off-season.*"

"*We all know that, Paul. That's why he's mentioned in this sequence. Willard, on the mound, has been inhuman, to say the least. He's struck down eleven straight Treadways. Little looks in for the sign from Alzebob. Benny has been a demon behind the plate, Paul.*"

"*He sure has, Ernie. Benny Alzebob has been playing like a man possessed. He's been gunning down runners all night.*"

"*Alzebob flashes Willard the sign, giving him a 666. He's calling for the hangman's curve! How does he do that?*"

"*I don't know, Ernie, I've only got four fingers, and he just put down eighteen!*"

"*It helps to be the Prince of Darkness, Paul. He's a devious one. Diablo, the second baseman, bluffs misery back to the bag. He's trying to keep him close in case of a base hit.*"

"*Diablo's been stealing souls left and right, Ernie. I think misery's trying to stay safe. That's not chalk out there. He spread blessed salt around the bag.*"

"*Little rocks back, gives his high-leg kick, and rolls ... here he comes! His wheelchair seems to stop at the plate! It's not a hangman's curve ... He served up a hanging curve! Jeremiah explodes his hands through the zone ... takes a mighty cut ... and drives it deep, way back! ... through the jugular ... its going! ... going! ... it's gone! Jeremiah Treadway has just taken Willard Little's head clean off his shoulders! The Treadways win the series!*

Laughing hysterically, self-realization sets in. I am truly insane! Here I am, on my way to kill someone, and I'm channeling Ernie Harwell. I can't stop laughing ... I'm so stupid ... what am I doing?! System of a Down's "Chop Suey!" erupts on my radio.

Now what? Is this a message from Willard? He knows I'm on my way?

"Once again, Jeremiah, you are asking the wrong questions." Ohhh, my arms are goose bumped like a mofo. "Turn and look at me. I assure you, I am real."

Slowly I turn.

"Jeremiah, it is good to see you again, alive."

"Well, if it isn't Mr. Gonnaleavemehanginlikeapieceofmeat D'Angelo. Get out of my car, slapdick."

Uh-oh, those Mediterranean blues are lookin' a bit pissed. Never seen Mr. D'Angelo look like this. Maybe I should apologize, or maybe I should kick his ass right out into the road! I've got the rage going again, and I'm ready to fight.

"Jeremiah, I must admit, you are trying my patience. No wonder our Father is ready to put you on waivers. In this game of life, you have played out your options."

"Look, Michael, once I'm done, I'll check myself into Northville State forever! Today, vengeance is mine, and no one else's!"

"Jeremiah, that is dangerous banter, and God has heard enough. You are not ready to take on Willard and *the Beast within*. Only with the help of your family will you be strong enough. You can't do this alone!"

"Okay, okay, you can go. I'll turn around and go back." Tell them what they want to hear ...

"Do not lie to me. I have been around your entire life. Fate has been on your side many times. Do we need to review? How many times have you sidestepped death?"

"What do you know about my life, Michael? I don't understand all this fateful life crap and avoiding death. I know that I've always had to take care of myself!"

"No, you haven't taken care of yourself, you've put yourself first! You have been selfish your whole life, always doing what *you* needed, never thinking of others! It has all come to this moment in time! God gave me the task of keeping you alive, as he had a plan. Even in all your illicit glory, you were saved, time and again."

"What in God's name are you talking about?"

"In God's name, I have been your protector. Through Your Valium overdose, the liquor and pills overdose, the acid incident, your impatience behind the wheel. You jumped the go and tried to pass. Do you think that truck truly missed you? When you hesitated at the light and the car blew the red at 60 mph? Even when you and your father were scheduled to die on the highway ... what do you think happened to that semi? You closed your eyes, and when you opened them? The truck disappeared. *The Beast within* tried to take your soul in the parking lot at the diner. Jeremiah, you had a gun to your head but did not pull the trigger. I was there, every time, to save you! I am Michael the Archangel, your protector! You wear me on your back. There is no such thing as a coincidence. Not everyone gets me as their guardian angel. I mean, dude, are you kidding me?"

Did he just say 'dude'? Michael the Archangel just used 'dude' in a sentence? That is so funny I may start laughing out loud.

"Jeremiah! Get out of your head and listen!"

"Your fateful lives have been used up, as has God's patience. If you go and face Willard now, you will die! *The Beast* has planned your death today. You are being given one last chance for fate to act in your favor, but you must show patience and an unselfish attitude. Go home, think about this, and learn to use your family to your advantage. You must do their bidding, as is God's will."

"But—"

He's gone again! I throw the stick in drive and jump on the gas. Screw it, I'm going after Willard! The dirt road starts rumbling under the jeep. The wheel is shaking in my hands. Whoa! Trees are swaying and leaves are flying everywhere.

The tallest building in the world sways, lightning crackles, and thunder echoes across the sand.

What has happened? I have not seen our Father like this in decades. There is much sorrow in heaven. The angels are crying in anguish.

"Michael!"

"Yes, my Father?"

"The unspeakable has happened. Willard and *the Beast within* have gone too far this time! They think they can flaunt their evil in my face? The scales have been tipped in their favor. They have murdered Rhona. You must go down and bring her to me."

"Yes, Father, but what of Jeremiah?"

"Fate has been altered—I have seen to it. What happens to Jeremiah is now *my* doing, not Lucifer's. God is always the home team, Michael. I get the last at bat, the final possession, the last line change! When this is over, good and evil will be balanced once again."

A giant clap roars across the sky! I slam on the brakes, and my jeep slides off the road. Coming to a halt, I check my shorts first. "What the shit was that?" My phone rings, and I see it's Cap. "Cap, did you just feel that thunder?"

"The whole county felt it, JT! But that's not why I called. Rhona is at the hospital … JT … she overdosed … Rho died on the table … they couldn't save her. I'm standing in the ER—"

"OD'd? What are you talking about? She doesn't do drugs!"

"Samari was on patrol when he spotted Mel's Vette rolling out of Hal's parking lot. He entered the diner and found Rho. She was knocked unconscious and shot up with heroin. Jeremiah, it's obvious that Mel and Willard were behind this."

This can't be happening … not my Sis. Tears are streaming down my cheeks. "Why didn't they hit her with Narcan?"

"So many people have been overdosing on heroin, the hospital ran out. They can only afford so much of the stuff. The drug companies are making a killing."

Big Pharma executives should all be in jail for taking advantage of this crisis. Between that and shoving their pills down America's throat, prison may be too nice of an option. Perhaps a bit of JT justice is warranted. We should take them and all their lobbyists, strap them to a table, and juice 'em up. Oops, we ran out of the remedy, cost is too high, so sorry, but please … enjoy your convulsions.

"JT, I need you to come back here right away."

A burning shade of evil wraps its arms around me, my soul scorched black forever. I'm left with a stain that can never be scrubbed clean. I've got nothing to lose, except for my life, and that's been up for the taking since I can remember. "Don't think so, Cap, got an errand to run."

"I know where you are, JT. My deputy tagged your jeep. Do not continue down this road. If Willard is back at the old Little cabin, *we* will apprehend him, not you!"

"Apprehend?" Forget telling them what they want to hear. "I'm gonna mash that little son of a bitch into a pile of flesh!"

A leaf being blown upward at the mercy of a gentle wind, slowly floating in midair … "Rhona Alastrina, take my hand."

"You look like JT's tattoo! Wait … where are we?"

"Our Father wants to see you."

"Oh my, you're Michael! St. Michael? Am I … Am I dead?"

"I was sent to bring you forth, but your fate is up to God. Not everyone gets an immediate audience. I believe your questions will soon be answered."

I slam the accelerator hard, imagining Willard's face under my boot. My jeep slides violently, side to side, as I get the adrenaline rush I've been waiting for. Sick Puppies, "You're Going Down," is jammin' in my head! I don't even realize my foot is still plastered to the pedal. Trees blend into a blur as my jeep careens out of control! I feel the rage … all thoughts turning singular … seeing myself shredding Willard into little bits!

"JT, slow down, brother … slow down!"

Chills spider-web out from the top of my shoulders, the tingling running down through my back.

"JT, this is not smart. Pull over—now is not the time. You're not ready …"

Oh, shit! My tires lose contact with the road. As I slam on the brakes, I hit a hole, spinning the jeep sideways. I do a snap 360, seeing the trees as one, engulfing me in a wooden tomb. Finally, I come to rest in the middle of the two-track. Breathing hard, my chest heaving, I can't believe my luck. Luck nothing. Fate smiled, death cheated. That was my brother's voice.

Jonathan, where did you go? How did I not smash my vehicle into the trees? I'm trying to focus, but my head is swimming in questions, half-thoughts ... I can't calm my brain. I shift my gaze ahead, and there it is, two hundred feet away, the cabin! I roll up and slip the jeep into park. It's time to give this skank a Godsmack!

Inside the cabin, two creatures of Lucifer revel in the misery of all that is transpiring.

He bows to the sickness as his phone rings. "My friend, this will be the trigger that brings about Jeremiah's demise."

"Talk to me, bitch."

"It's done. She's dead."

Willard's eyes roll back into his head, as slithering gray mucous oozes out of the corners. Articulated jaws unlock, while he wraps his head around the news. Moaning like a two-bit whore, he has found his release. "Mmmm, Melchiah. My sweet, deranged Melchiah, you have served us well."

The clouds steamroll the sun, bringing a deeper shade of darkness to Willard's cabin. The giant black oozing maggots gather into form. The feeding frenzy over, the shadow lets out its own guttural moan.

"I can hear the sounds of approval. I had the time of my life! A girl could get used to this. Who's next on our agenda?"

"I'm sending you on a mission. Your demon state will bear fruition upon completing the task."

"What is it that you need me to do?"

"You need to continue to harvest the souls of the living. The more you gorge, the stronger your darkness will grow. Through the pain of others, you will morph into the Black Queen. *The Beast within* will guide your way. Then ... I need you to find my son."

CHAPTER 20

"Rhona Alastrina Cairstine MacVicar."

The voice is deep, resonant, and warm ... so very warm. Life is making sense now, strength growing like a fertile seed. Do answers await? "Yes, my Father?"

"Look down and tell me what you see."

"I'm lying in bed at the hospital. Am I in the ER? Why is no one moving? Lord, have I died?"

"You have been used as a pawn by Lucifer. I have temporarily slowed time. Willard and *the Beast within* are trying to sway the balance. I will no longer tolerate their hatred. They are both evil creatures, and fate will not treat them pleasantly. Being a defender of the people and a follower of the Trinity, there is a place here for you. The choice is yours and yours alone—to stay or return."

"My Father, this is everything I ever imagined. I don't want to disappoint You but ..."

"Rhona Alastrina, there is nothing you can do that would disappoint. What does your heart tell you?"

"I must go back. JT needs me. Yes ... I have to go back!"

God broadens his face into a smile that would make the sunset jealous. "Jeremiah's li'l Braveheart,' my earthbound angel, always putting others first. Your work for me is not yet finished, and you have power

121

not yet understood. Stay by Jeremiah's side and guide him. He must be one with his family, and from there you will know which direction to go. Learn to use the gifts I have granted you … and use them indeed, as you must."

"My Father, I will not let you down."

"Michael, escort Rhona back to the living.

I've come this far, and now I'm not so sure I should go in there. How many chances does one man get? Willard's had me on the run, always one step ahead. Everything's been on his terms but that can change. JT, do this for your family, for your parents, your brother.

"This is as far as I go."

"But what do I do? How will I wake up? I overdosed, and they all think I'm dead."

"Rhona Alastrina, lie down and take your place. Be ready for astonishment, as it will be all around you. You have been clinically deceased for over four minutes. When you feel ready, open your eyes."

"Captain!"

"Go ahead, base, over."

"Captain, you're not going to believe this, but Rhona is alive!"

"Base, repeat please."

"Captain! She effin woke up!"

"Are you drunk, Samari? I just walked out of the hospital after Doc called time of death!"

"I swear, Captain, she just came to—she's smiling. When Rhona sat up, the nurse screamed so loud that Doc 'bout had a heart attack." The deputy pauses, his tone turning to amazement. "But that's not the weirdest part, Captain."

Cappy, already having his mind blown, can barely speak. "What … what do you mean?"

"While this was happening, Jake's kid was brought in DOA from an apparent overdose."

"Oh, my God, please no … not Jake's kid … oh my God …"

"Wait, Captain, there's more …" Sammy almost can't continue.

"Deputy! What the heck are you talking about?"

"Rhona, sir. She went over to the body, said it wasn't his time … something about balance. Captain. Rho placed one hand on his head and one on his heart. She closed her eyes, and his opened! Jim said he's never seen anything like it! Doc mumbled something about God and Fate smiling. He's been hugging her like crazy! Never seen Doc this elated."

"Did Rhona say anything?"

"She said you have to stop Jeremiah. Rhona's adamant about JT dying if you can't stop him. She said he's heading for Little's old cabin and Willard knows he's coming. It's about two klicks north of JT's property."

"I know, Samari. I'm about ten minutes out. What else?"

"Jake said he saw Mel's Vette screaming away, down the road, right before he found his son."

"Put out a BOLO, Sammy. Note she's a suspected serial killer. This is almost turning …" Cap hesitates, looking for the right words.

"Biblical, Captain."

"Come back, Deputy?"

"That's what Doc said. This is turning Biblical."

"Did Doc say anything else?"

"Yes, sir. If you and JT make it back alive, he's opening that hundred-year-old bottle of scotch."

Do it for Sis. That skank deserves to die an excruciating death. A feeling starts to tingle in my heels. Haunting resolve streams its way up my legs. Seeds of anger plant themselves in my darkest recesses. The whisper of adrenaline bubbles slowly, spiraling its way through my spine. My heart responds, doing its job, pumping anger directly into my pleasure center. I can taste sweet vengeance dripping off my tongue. I glance down and fixate on the sword. Wrapping my hand around the handle, I feel the power of vengeance. To hell with everything and everyone. I'm doing this for me! Getting out of the jeep, I head directly for the front door.

I'm ten feet from redemption.

Do I sneak in?

Would a badass sneak around, JT?

He knows you're here, dumbass. You've seen all the movies. *Just bust in there like a man!*

The adrenaline is screaming through every cell in my body. The sword in my hand, melding mind and soul … every bit of moral fiber now decayed. Is this the power of twelve or the sickness of one?

What's that smell? A sweetness trickles up from under the front door, its wispy tendrils of ecstasy winding their way into my brain.

The door cracks open, emitting a rusty creak.

The irresistible aroma of days past caresses my face, sickly enticing smoke catapulting my brain into a fit of frenzied desire. Opium! Whaaat? All thoughts of vengeance gone, muscle memory taking the lead, I feel the sword dangling, like that of Damocles, holding my head hostage.

My body blindly follows my addictions into the dimly lit den. Saliva glands erupting, the taste is almost mine … and then it's gone! The cloud in my brain clears. I've dropped the weapon and am standing well inside the cabin. The smell of damp wood and mold now becomes my reality. What just happened?

The door creaks again as it shuts.

A voice slithers out of the darkness. "Welcome, Jeremiah, I was expecting you."

Frozen in time, hurdling myself into my head, I attempt to escape. I'm back in the carriage, leaving the church and heading to the graveyard. The church bells are thundering through my head, clashing with the sound of the hooves striking the pavement … Dave is … *klippityclop klippitty klippityclop* … dead … *klippityclop klippitty klippityclop* … Dave is … *klippityclop klippitty klippityclop* … dead … I'm standing over his grave, praying for forgiveness, tears of regret washing down my own denial. "Please, God, there has to be room in Heaven for my friend. People can't always handle what's been thrust upon them. Suicide needs to be understood, not scorned."

"Ahh, weak until the end, Jeremiah? Begging God to let your friend in? You should be asking for yourself." Willard rolls closer. "Because I'm going to make sure you die an excruciatingly slow death!"

"I'm not leaving without your head in my hand." I'm swept by visions of generations past, my family extinguished, assassinated by this freak show of Littles. My heart pumps with an increasing rhythm as my brain cultivates adrenaline. How do I step back and grab the sword? If this were *Resident Evil* I could do a backflip, pick it up, and send it flying like a double-edged boomerang! It would lop off Willard's head and come full circle to my hand while the head flopped, bounced, and rolled to my feet. Looking around, not finding Mila, I guess plan B will have to work. "I'm almost within an arm's reach of your throat. What's to keep me from breaking your fucking neck?"

"This!"

Self-hatred pounds me to my knees! Anxiety and guilt shove me face-first into the wooden floor! Starting to wish I had a plan C.

"I can put you into withdrawal any time I want, a gift to me from *the Beast within*! Do you feel anguish kicking you in the gut? Is your skin rolling off your limbs? Your brain is molting your body … like a reptilian junkie!"

Willard is sitting over me, both screaming and laughing, narcissism piling on top of arrogance. "I control you! You are mine to dispose of, any way I choose. This is my territory, my world, to take whatever I want! I will take your soul and give it to *the Beast within*. You will enter our darkness! The Light you so desperately crave has been pissed all over. I'm going to leave you in pain, this state of misery, while I relish this moment. When you no longer amuse me, you will join your family in death."

In the fetal position … again? My last headbang? I feel so sick, the flu times West Nile. Can't stop shaking, the duel begins. The choice of pistols has been made, with body and mind pacing off against each other. Unyielding despair, nausea, writhing guilt, retching cramps, self-loathing! Sweating and shaking. God, please end this! I don't want to be here anymore.

"We finally get there, eh, Mr. Jeremiah Treadway? You're weak! You haven't helped yourself, do you think God will help you? Do you think God cares about you? We put that li'l whore, Rhona, down like a stray animal. She took the plunge, and now you're next! God loses, you lose, your family has lost!"

Through my unending haze, I hear something click, like a hammer being pulled back. I lurch over and look up.

"Well, well, well, my loser daughter has returned."

This break in Willard's concentration is allowing me to catch my breath. I now see Tracey standing ten feet away, pointing the biggest effin gun I've ever seen straight at Willard's head.

"My .44 Magnum? That thing will knock you on your ass. You don't have the nerve! You're a spineless coward, just like your mother!"

What is happening here? Wait ... did he say daughter? Have I just stepped into a bad PCP trip? I'm trying to crawl forward but swear I'm moving back. As I move, my vision narrows, and they're zooming further away!

"Oh, my sweet darling daughter. Looks like I'm going to have to give you the beating you deserve!"

"You destroyed my mother! You've torn me down for the last time!"

Tracey's hands are shaking like she's scared to death. I can't believe she's related to this skank. Think about that, dude. You were doing Willard's daughter. Snap back, JT! You can't let her live with the image of her father's head exploding. She has a good soul, you could feel it.

"Tracey, please, you won't be able to live with this. It's not worth shooting this scum. Protect your conscience, protect your soul! Let him do what he needs to me ... turn and run, now!"

"Aww, Jeremiah has a soft spot for my daughter? Not thinking about himself for a change? Put the gun down, Ms. Gutless Wonder. When I'm done here, I'm going to give you what you got coming. Then," Willard pauses for the dark, evil drama, "your brother will be all mine!"

I hear the siren, a car come to a sliding halt, a door slam. Cappy, I know that's you. Hurry the eff up.

"My Lord, I can't bear to watch. This can't be happening! What of fate?"

"Jeremiah has done the unexpected, putting aside selfishness for someone else, offering up his life so that Tracey may live. He has taken a first step. Michael, fate is about to unfold!"

The front door explodes into splinters as Cappy rushes in.

Willard throws his head back laughing, as if the joke's on us. "I'll be found insane, unable to stand trial!"

His laughter is cut off by a deafening *boom*.

The world around me is thrust into stop motion. I see the bullet track as it blows out the back of Willard's skull. The concussion of the blast slams into my eardrums, as I'm hit with a sonic silence. Unable to hear, I see Cappy frantically mouthing something. He's pointing his Glock at Tracey, who was launched back into the wall after pulling the trigger. Now she's sitting up, and Trace has got the Mag leveled at Cap! There's this crazy look in Cappy's eyes, something I've never seen before … terror! I'm trying to yell at Tracey, but I can't hear anything. I don't even know if sound is coming out of my mouth. I spin around and see Willard's brain splattered across the far wall, looking like someone blended up a sausage pizza and sprayed it everywhere. I lean away, dry heaving, sickened by the sight.

"Drop the weapon! Tracey, please! Don't make me pull the trigger!"

Trace lowers the gun. My body slumps back down, relief flowing over me like the first tab of Suboxone I ever experienced. Cappy's words start penetrating the slop in my head.

"Tracey, sweetie," Cap continues, his gun still staring her down, "you've been abused, beaten, and threatened your whole life. We'll get you the help you need. But, sweetie, please drop the weapon. We can all go home, but you have to let go of the gun."

Tracey's eyes wander around the room. She takes in the view of her father's body, with only parts of his face and neck remaining. Trace stops and gazes into my eyes. They're touching deep inside me, like a hurt puppy, wanting only to be loved. Tracey mouths, "*Please forgive me, JT. I'm so sorry.*" She spins the gun, barrel up under her chin, pulls the hammer back, and looks at Cappy. "I can't live with this!"

Cap yells, "No!" as I dive away, covering my ears.

I can't look ... won't look ... can't make me. I hear Cappy sobbing. This man has seen death up close and personal before. He served courageously in the Marines, and this is too much even for him. I think it would be best if I just laid here and never got up. If this is the world as is, I don't want to be a part of it. My soul has been charred beyond all recognition. I'm deep into my own abyss, plated armor surrounding me, unable to be reached again. This is my end? Catatonic for life. I can see it now. They drag me out, lay me in a bed, stick a tube in my arm. Never blinking, lost in my head, till death do I part.

"JT. JT, open your eyes."

That's not Michael's voice. Guess he was benched in favor of ... Gabriel? Yes, this must be Gabriel, come to escort me to the ferryman. Maybe he can front me a couple of coins to get across the River. I'm sure Heaven isn't waiting.

"JT, open your damn eyes." I hear laughter. "I need some help with this joint. I've been looking for the Light, but I can't find it."

I know that laugh! The voice. I can't effin believe it! I bolt straight up.

"Dave!" He's not here. I know what I heard. Look up, Dave, look up. God, it's time. Please give him your hand!

Okay, maybe catatonic was the way to go, wouldn't have to cop to insanity. I haven't resolved the issue of my own issues. Looking around, reality setting back in, my thoughts turn to Tracey. I think she realized abuse begets abuse. Her environment brainwashed her, muscle memory taking over, abuse turning into a default mechanism. "Jeremiah, let's get out of this cabin."

I've seen Cap look better, but at least we're both still standing. "Yeah, Cap, I'm with ya on that."

CHAPTER 21

After walking out of a scene that would make Quentin Tarantino blush, we're both greeted by a stunning sight. The cabin faces due west, and the message presented is not lost on either of us. The sky is a blending array of yellows, oranges, and reds. Wispy clouds are brushed throughout. Mediterranean blue runs across the horizon. The orange mixes its way up, on both sides of the sun, as if hands were reaching into the sky.

"JT, there's a sunset that might make even God Himself jealous."

"Cappy, I'd like to believe it's God smiling down on Siam."

I plop down on the top step, and Cappy follows suit. "JT, you look like hell, not even warmed over."

"Cap, I can't even explain, but Willard put me straight into withdrawal. He had me. I was about to die. Tracey saved my life."

"Should have told you more about the Little family, Jeremiah, I'm sorry. This has been going on for generations. Your dad didn't want you involved."

"Why didn't you warn me about that psycho bitch, Melchiah? Please tell me you put a bullet in her forehead."

Cappy stands up and kicks at the ground. "She's going to be a whole other problem, JT."

"She got away?" My gut twists. It wasn't supposed to be a rhetorical question, but it's met with silence. "Eugene, I swear I've got a guardian angel. He's been appearing to me for months. Thought I was hallucinating, but Michael is real." Is Cap buying this?

"Jeremiah, you've been ducking death your whole life. That is not unbelievable."

"That's only half of it, Cap. The voices I've been hearing are my family. Jonathan was trying to warn me when I was heading here."

"Your brother and family loved you very much. Jonathan knew all about the curse. He was intent on bringing Willard down. I didn't much believe in the manifestation of evil until lately. My belief in God has been emboldened throughout this whole mess."

"I've been struggling, Cappy. Too much has happened to make me think I'm really nuts."

"Jeremiah, I don't believe you're crazy. With everything I've experienced over the last 30 years, this actually makes sense." Cap hesitates, then laughs. "Now maybe that makes me crazy too, but I know I'm in good company." Cappy sits back down and throws his arm around my shoulder. "JT, I love you like a son. You can lean on me forever."

This should make me feel better, but I'm lost in sorrow. My mind's adrift on the sea of despair. The final gut-punch delivered by life … my li'l punk rocker, my Sissy, taken by the hands of evil. My head drops between my knees, and I start bawling. "JT, easy. It's over. It's going to be all right."

"Rhona." I can barely get the words out. "Rhona is gone."

"Ohhh shit, JT, no. We really didn't have time for idle chat when I kicked the door in. I'm sorry, Jeremiah, I didn't have time to tell you. She's—"

Vehicles roll up, with one coming to a flying stop, interrupting Cap. I'm not listening, crawling deeper into the closet, intent on shutting the door.

"She's alive, Jeremiah. Rho freaked the whole ER staff out, including Doc, and regained consciousness."

Whaaaat? I spring straight up. There, standing in front of me, is the most beautiful thing I have ever seen. The smile I'm looking at had to be placed there by angels.

We both scream, in unison, "WHAAAT!" Rho jumps straight into my arms, 'bout knocking me on my ass.

"I thought you were dead."

"Guess not, J-man!"

We push each other away, staring into each other's eyes with a child's astonishment … and let fly with another, "WHAAAT!"

"Bitch, you flatlined!"

"Well, I was sent back to cover your sorry ass."

Rho's looking at me, trying to muffle her laughter, but can't keep it in. "I crack myself up, JT."

"Hey, that's my line!" We both bust it out, giggling uncontrollably, driven by elation on top of relief. "So, did you see the Light? God? What did He say?"

"My heightened senses are a gift. God gave me these abilities. He said," Rhona starts blushing, "I'm his 'earthbound angel.'"

A sense of peace washes over her face. Sissy's aura seems to glow with warmth. "We're going to work, together, with your family. I'm going to help you to understand their message."

Not gonna lie, I'm a little scared. Mel must have crawled back under the rock from whence she came. And I know *the Beast within* is still out there. Still, it would be nice to hear from my family. I feel good about the twelve of us working together, outing the skanks of the world and keeping the balance. It does have a nice ring: we are twelve.

"Hold on, J-man, if you are twelve, where does that leave me?"

"Rhona Alastrina Cairstine, you're the Guiding Light!"

"Ooh, I like that." A broad grin forms. "But where does this leave you?"

Lost in a brief thought, scanning the horizon, I place an arm around Rho. I lean in close. "Clean. This leaves me clean and moving forward."

CHAPTER 22

"Interesting move. You have some experience with this game, I see."

"You play a textbook game Yourself … ancient text, I expect."

God, laughing heartily, gains the attention of the angels. They have been singing in unison since witnessing the sunset below. St. Peter stands patiently off to the side, having escorted a new arrival from the Gates.

"I'll be with you in a moment, Peter. Please forgive my manners, but our most recent soul to enter is giving me quite a match."

Michael, now watching intently, seems to be getting some pleasure from this.

Unable to stifle His own laughter, our Father continues, "Michael, are you rooting against God?"

"My Lord, you have beaten me 4,768 times in a row, but still, I would never want to see you lose. I could, maybe, possibly be rooting for our new brother to win." Michael cannot hide his enormous smile, and neither can God.

"God being humbled? I'll take it under advisement." Even the stoic St. Peter can't hide his laughter, knowing full well that God always gets the last move.

"I'm sorry for taking so long to find my way here, my Father. Somehow I was pushed in the right direction."

"My son, no apologies necessary, it takes some longer than others to find the Light. Many prayed for you, some more than others, and I listened. I heard the vehement cries of one, and so I allowed a bit of interference. That push was my warrior Michael guiding your fate. And I could not allow your friend Jeremiah, after shedding one of his demons, to waste away. Welcome to heaven, David!"

God looks to Peter. "Please bring over our new arrival."

Our Father is swept over by such empathy that it brings Michael to tears. "My sweet child, it brought me much sorrow to watch your life unfold. You were dealt a horrible hand, yet you remain such a caring soul. I cannot hold you responsible for the end of your physical life on Earth. Against all odds, you maintained your morality. David, please step forth."

Michael's heart swells with anticipation. An unseen force slowly pushes the drapes open. The angels stop singing and perch on the front row. Even St. Peter is now sneaking a peek over their wings. "Let me introduce you two, and then you can show her around. Dave, please greet our newest arrival. Welcome to Heaven, Tracey!"

The angels go back to singing, as this is what they do when they're happy. St. Peter heads back to the Gates of Pearl to await the next fateful soul. St. Michael goes back to the grinding wheel to sharpen his slayer of demons, knowing the next mission is just on the horizon. God, it seems, has another morsel of wisdom to share. "Dave, one more thing."

"Yes, my Father?"

"Checkmate."

THANK YOU

Therapy for the soul comes in many forms. Finding the right path can be elusive. Thank you for joining me in my wayward trek toward redemption. Find me at my website danielthomasjr.com and share your path with me.

WANT MORE?

Did you like this book? Ha, who am I kidding, of course you did!

And that's good, because I'm just getting started.

You can stay connected with me at www.danielthomasjr.com and sign up to be notified when the next release is available. By signing up now, you will be first in line for exclusive deals and giveaways.

Even better, the **first chapter of my next book** will be yours for free. Yep, totally free, and I will send it right to your inbox (as soon as I finish penning it of course).

What are you waiting for?

A QUICK FAVOR PLEASE?

Before you go can I ask you for a quick favor?

Would you please leave me a review on Amazon?

Reviews are very important for authors like me, as they help us reach more people. This will in turn enable me to write more books for you.

So, please do me a solid and leave a review today using whatever platform you are reading on. It is quick and painless and will only take a second.

Thank you for reading, and thank you so much for being part of this adventure.

-Dan

ABOUT THE AUTHOR

Dan smoked his first cigarette at ten, had his first drink at eleven, and smoked weed at fourteen. He experimented with every drug known to mankind. Sharp, hard hitting, and raw. Dan shares his unique perspective derived from a four-decade journey through addiction. Written in a fictional setting, join him in his search for redemption as he struggles with the dark, the light, and everything in between. Dan currently resides in Plymouth, MI with his girlfriend, stepson, dog and cat. He's fascinated with the paranormal and loves his loud music therapy, baseball and college football, but his sons are what truly make his world go 'round.

Made in the USA
Middletown, DE
01 December 2017